Back to the Heartbreak

Ava Mitchell

Copyright © 2024 by [Author or Pen Name]

All rights reserved.

No portion of this book may be reproduced in any form without written permission from the publisher or author, except as permitted by U.S. copyright law.

Contents

1. Chapter 1 — 1
2. Chapter 2 — 9
3. Chapter 3 — 18
4. Chapter 4 — 27
5. Chapter 5 — 36
6. Chapter 6 — 43
7. Chapter 7 — 55
8. Chapter 8 — 65
9. Chapter 9 — 74
10. Chapter 10 — 83
11. Chapter 11 — 94
12. Chapter 12 — 100
13. Chapter 13 — 115
14. Chapter 14 — 127
15. Chapter 15 — 144

16.	Chapter 16	156
17.	Chapter 17	168
18.	Chapter 18	175
19.	Chapter 19	183
20.	Chapter 20	198
21.	Epilogue	207

Chapter 1

"How could you do this to me, Katie?" The sorrow was evident in Scarlet's voice as she quickly stepped away from the bed where her girlfriend lay naked. Katie quickly covered herself with the gray duvet, looking at Scarlet.

"I-It's not what it looks like." Katie spoke as she began to get off the bed where she was laying with the guy she just had sex with.

"Bullshit." Scarlet spat as she ran a hand through her hair and tried to stop tears from falling out of her eyes.

"You told me, you were gonna work today and you're here doing....." Scarlet shook her head as she threw away the bouquet that she had in her hand. Katie had tears welling up in her eyes as well as she looked at the girl she hurt.

"I'm sorry." Katie bowed her head down which made Scarlet more furious as she glanced at the guy who was still in bed, staring at Scarlet with a smirk. When Scarlet looked at him carefully, she realized who it was.

Her fists clenched as she tightened her jaw, her eyes that were now filled with hurt and sorrow turned black. She didn't want to stay in the same room with the two as she stumbled back to get out of there. Katie began to step close to Scarlet but the other girl quickly raised her hand as to stop the girl from even coming close to her.

Scarlet turned around and left the apartment with quick steps as she was finding it hard to breathe in there.

She was stumbling every now and then but that didn't stop her from quickly walking to her own apartment. The air was cold as it blew past her, the busy street of New York was filled with people as she kept bumping into them.

No sorry, no nothing was said as the strangers would glare at her. She had tears running down her eyes as she felt lost in the well recognized street. Nothing felt the same, and certainly not her heart which didn't want to beat anymore.

She looked up into the slowly darkening sky and wondered what she had done wrong to get this punishment. She wondered what she had done wrong to feel this kind of immense pain that didn't want to leave. She wondered, and cried as she walked with quick steps towards her apartment she called home.

Katie had her head in her hands when she felt the presence of Stewart beside her, she looked up at him with a glare as he kept up his smirk.

"Do you even know what has just happened?" Katie hissed as she threw him the worst glare she could muster. "Yeah, I finally know where I had seen you before."

A laugh escaped Stewart's mouth as Katie felt more tears streaming down her face.

"This is your fault, she hates me. She'll never forgive me." Katie mumbled sadly as the guy beside her shook his head with a smirk.

"If I remember correctly, you were the one that ripped my shirt off first."

"You could've stopped me, at least then I wouldn't have broken her heart." She spat as she stood up to leave her own bedroom.

Stewart harshly grabbed her arm before he stood up to look into her eyes with a sharp look.

"Don't you dare put this all on me, okay? You came on to me." He harshly spoke as he gripped her arm tightly. "And besides, you better make everything okay with her. I am not in the position to lose my best editor."

He let her arm go and smirked as he fixed his tie, "Bye, Katie." He gave her a final smirk before he walked out of the room and out of the apartment, leaving Katie alone.

Katie had tears flowing from her eyes because she already knew that she couldn't fix anything with Scarlet. No one wants to get back together with someone that cheated on them.

The next day, when Stewart stepped foot in his office, his secretary ran inside his office with a envelope in her hand. Stewart gave her a questioning look to which she handed him the envelope before apologizing.

"What's this?" Stewart asked as he sat on his leather chair, gripping the envelope gently.

"Ms. Payne came to the office earlier and gave this envelope to the receptionist, saying to give it to you when you came in. I didn't open it." His secretary spoke while fixing her glasses on the bridge of her nose.

Stewart's eyes went a bit wide before he quickly ripped off the opening of the envelope, he unfolded the paper that sat in the envelope and immediately regretted his actions of yesterday.

He stood up from his chair abruptly, throwing the paper on his huge mahogany desk and rubbed his forehead. What sat on his desk was a resignation letter. Not any resignation letter but a resignation letter from Stewart's best editor, Scarlet Payne.

Scarlet sat in the plane with her eyes swollen and red from all the crying she did last night, with all the crying came the thinking. She thought about what she should do to go away from all the things that gave her happiness before but now, they all reminded her of a relationship that ended with the worst possible thing happening. Being cheated on.

She sighed when the announcements began, to buckle seat belts and turn off all phones. She closed her eyes as she thought about how her family would react to this surprise homecoming.

She was scared of their reactions but most of all, she was relieved to leave New York, that only gave her dreams and then heartbreak.

"We will be reaching Greenville, North Carolina in about four hours, please buckle your seat belts." The pilot's voice came from the intercom as Scarlet looked out the window, watching the plane about to take flight.

She was going to meet her family and maybe stay with her family, but there was only one problem. She didn't know how to tell them that she got her heartbroken by a girl because her family had no idea that she is gay.

Stewart sat stressed out in his leather chair as he kept rubbing his forehead. He had no idea that what he would do would backfire this much, if he knew he would've never slept with Scarlet's girlfriend.

He kept mumbling to himself about what he would do now. His glass door opened and he saw a familiar face, which made him more stressed out.

"Good morning." Lauren, Stewart's sister greeted with a huge smile as she came in the room with her handbag on her shoulder.

Stewart didn't even reply as he looked away from the girl and on the page that held the names of the people that could become an editor if he just gave them a chance.

"Wow, someone has a sour mood." The blonde girl spoke with a pout as she sat in the chair that was in front of her brother's desk.

"I didn't even see Scarlet when I came here today, did she take a leave today?" Lauren asked as she looked at her brother with her intense emerald eyes.

"She left." Stewart looked up at his sister who had a frown on her face. "What do you mean?"

"She left, permanently. She just gave me a resignation letter and left." Stewart ranted as he stood up from his leather chair, to pace around his office.

"But, why?" Lauren asked as she frowned deeply, she didn't know why but she felt a sudden rush of fear....?

"I slept with her girlfriend." Stewart spoke quietly which was barely audible and his sister gave him a look to repeat what he said.

He sighed, knowing that one way or another she might find out what happened, "I slept with her girlfriend."

Lauren shook her head disappointingly at her brother and stood up from her seat.

"I didn't mean to, she just came on to me." Stewart explained himself which just went to deaf ears as Lauren gave him a look.

"And you didn't have the decency to stop her or better yet, stop yourself." Lauren spoke loudly which immediately made her brother bow his head down in guilt.

"She would be so broken." Lauren spoke in concern as she imagined what the girl would've been feeling, being cheated on and with her boss.

"You have to help me, Laur." Stewart begged as he came closer to his sister. "I need her, she's my best editor."

Lauren rolled her eyes at her brother, "It's all about money for you, you don't understand her grief."

"Please, just go talk to her or something. I promise, I'll repay you with ice cream." Stewart pleaded as he placed his hands on her shoulders.

"I want a vanilla sundae." Lauren spoke as she began to walk out of her brother's office.

"Whatever you like, baby sis." Stewart loudly spoke as Lauren made her way out of his office.

"She said, something about going back to her hometown." The landlord said as he counted the dollar bills he had scored from the questioning blonde.

"Where's her hometown?" The inquiring blonde asked as she looked at the man with a glare.

"My mind's a bit foggy..." Lauren quickly set another dollar on his palm with a sigh, making the man smile wider.

"Greenville, North Carolina." The man answered happily as he looked at the blonde.

"Any address?" The man was about to say something when the blonde again placed a dollar bill in the man's hand.

"I don't know of any addresses but thanks for the dollar anyway." The man happily spoke, making the blonde roll her eyes, before he began to walk back inside his apartment.

"Wait." Lauren spoke up and the man turned to look at her with a confused look on his face.

"How was she when she left?" The man was a bit startled from the question but his face immediately softened when he saw the gentle and concerned look on the blonde's face.

"Not good, she didn't even smile at me when she gave me the advance rent money for two months. Her eyes were all red and puffy, I think she was crying all night." Lauren's face held concern as she thanked the man with a small smile and turned around to leave.

Lauren could not imagine the pain that Scarlet had felt but she could easily imagine the suffering since, she too, had her heartbroken once.

"Do you know where her parents live?" Lauren asked her brother on the phone as she packed up her clothes in a luggage bag.

"Why, what happened?" Stewart asked from the other side, as he sipped some coffee.

"She left New York this morning, going to Greenville." Lauren answered as she placed her red dress in the bag as well.

"She what!?" Stewart exclaimed as he spit his coffee all over his desk.

"I need the home address, Art." Lauren spoke impatiently as she zipped up her bag, now packed up.

"But what are you going to do with it?" Stewart asked as he ordered his secretary to get Scarlet's file while cleaning his mouth with a wet wipe.

"I'm going to get her back, that's what." Lauren spoke into her phone as she packed up her laptop as well.

"I didn't know you would go to these lengths just for an ice cream sundae." Stewart spoke with a laugh as he began to tell her the address. Stewart gestured his secretary to clean up the mess on his table.

Lauren wrote the address in a notebook before she bid goodbye to her brother, hanging up the phone.

She sighed as she knew that she wasn't doing this all for an ice cream sundae anymore. But why else was she doing this, even she couldn't understand.

Chapter 2

"Do you need anything else?" The air hostess asked Lauren with a smile plastered on her face. Lauren replied with a shake of her head.

The air hostess left Lauren to her thoughts as she looked out of the plane, at the clouds.

The pilot had announced that they would be arriving in Greenville in half an hour, Lauren was scared of what Scarlet might say about this but she knew that it wouldn't be nice.

Even if Lauren treated Scarlet with respect, she was still the sister of the man that slept with Scarlet's girlfriend, and this made Lauren a little scared.

Scarlet was sat in her old house, on her old couch, in front of her old parents, with a frown on her face.

"I can't believe that Vanessa is getting married and you didn't even send me an invite." She was pissed off to say the least as her parents smiled apologetically at her. She rolled her eyes at them, when Vanessa entered the living room, talking to her fiancee on Skype.

"Say hi to mom and dad, Kevin." Vanessa spoke happily as she brought her phone in front of her parents, completely ignoring her younger and only sister.

"Hi, Kevin." Laura, Mrs. Payne, greeted with a smile and a wave as she wanted to avoid the awkward situation with her younger daughter at best.

Mr Payne, Andrew, followed his wife's lead as he greeted Kevin with an overly excited tone of voice, making it obvious that he disliked the man.

Vanessa took the phone away from her parents faces and began to make kissy faces at her fiance, through her phone.

Scarlet had no energy left to even discuss about this with her parents anymore, so she just got off the couch with an angry look.

"I'm just gonna be in my room." She grumbled as she began to take her luggage upstairs but was stopped by her parents' voice.

"About that....." Her father paused as he nudged his wife to explain, while Scarlet stood impatiently on the first step of the stairs.

"Vanessa is staying in your room." Laura spoke with an apologetic smile, the fiftieth one in the last three hours.

"I'll take the guest room, then." Scarlet spoke, controlling her anger.

"Yeah, that's for your relatives that are coming for Van's wedding." Laura played with her fingers as the same smile stayed on her face, while Scarlet went red.

"Great, where am I gonna go now?" Scarlet questioned as she looked at her parents with a glare.

"Oh, you can stay with me in my room." Vanessa spoke from the recliner as she still had her cellphone in her hand.

'Not your room, my room.' Scarlet bitterly thought as she gave her sister a tight lipped smile before climbing up the stairs to go to Vanessa's room.

The cab driver gave Lauren her change before he drove off, while Lauren straightened up to look at the medium sized house colored white while all the other houses on the street were sky blue.

She dragged her bag by the wheels to the front door and rang the bell with sweaty hands. She didn't know why she was so afraid of what might happen. She quickly wiped her hands on her dress that she also straightened out nervously.

Voices could be heard from the inside of the house as she prepared herself for what was to come. The door opened and she gave a bright smile to the little boy that stood in the doorway looking up at her.

He stared at her, still standing in the doorway, making her uncomfortable to say the least. "Um, hi. Is Scarlet here?" The boy instantly gave her a toothy grin before taking her hand and dragging her in.

"Aunty Scar, there's someone here to meet you!" The boy exclaimed while Lauren rolled her bag in the house wearing the best smile she could muster.

'I'm about to meet her parents.' She thought as if it was such a big deal.

As the boy neared the living room, the chatter became more clear and she was ready to face the family.

"Oh, who is this, young man?" An old woman came into view and she smiled at Lauren before bringing her gaze to the little boy holding her hand.

"She's here to meet Aunty Scar." The boy spoke excitedly making him look more adorable as the woman smiled at the sight.

The woman bent down to be level with the little boy, "Why don't you go call her from upstairs?" The boy nodded frantically before running to go up the stairs.

"Hi, I'm the birth giver of Scarlet." The woman held out her hand for the blonde to shake, which she did quickly with a small smile. "You can call me Laura."

"Lauren. Lauren Grayson." The woman smiled and beckoned Lauren toward the sofa, where another woman sat, talking to her phone animatedly.

"This is my oldest daughter, Vanessa." Laura introduced Vanessa to Lauren, who wasn't aware of her surroundings. "She's busy talking to her fiancee, they're getting married next month." Laura spoke with a smile as she gestured Lauren to sit beside the bride-to-be.

Laura sat down, herself, on the recliner as Lauren placed her luggage beside her and her purse, on her lap. "So, how do you know Scarlet?" Laura asked as she stared at the girl.

"Oh, we-" Lauren was cut off when she heard the familiar voice of Scarlet, which made her nervousness come back in full force as she stared at the entrance of the living room.

"Who is it?" Scarlet asked her cousin, Gregory, for the millionth time in that minute as he dragged her by the hand towards the living room.

She rolled her eyes when she got no response from the six year old. She was busy drowning in her sorrows in Vanessa's room when the six year old barged in and dragged her out. Katie was still swirling in the black headed's mind and it didn't make it any better that her heart kept telling her to go back to the girl.

Finally, the two cousins reached the living room and what sat there- who sat there- made her blood boil. Lauren quickly stood up forgetting about the purse that sat in her lap as it fell, she smiled nervously at Scarlet before picking it up. Scarlet glared at the 21 year old, while Lauren knew what was going to happen next.

"Can we talk outside for a moment?" Scarlet spoke sickeningly sweet as she looked at her mother for the permission.

Laura glanced from Lauren to Scarlet before she shrugged her shoulders nonchalantly.

Scarlet came closer to Lauren and grabbed her wrist a little too tightly that made Lauren wince, but it didn't stop the black headed woman that was just waiting to explode.

She dragged Lauren outside, and away from her family, as she closed the front door behind her so that no one would hear her loud voice. She took a deep breath as Lauren soothed her wrist with a frown.

"What are you doing here?" Scarlet managed to ask the girl calmly as she kept her anger at bay.

"I-"

"No, don't answer that. I already know why." Scarlet cut Lauren off as she sarcastically spoke. "Stewart wants me back, doesn't he?"

Lauren was lost for words as she tried to calm her heart from exploding in fear of the once sweet and caring woman.

"Just go back and tell him that even if he begs me to come back, I won't. I'm through with him, his magazine and everything." Scarlet spoke a little too loudly making Lauren flinch and bow her head down.

Lauren was about to speak when the front door opened and Laura came out wearing a frown on her face.

"Oh, my baby." She engulfed Scarlet in a hug as Lauren stared at the two in confusion. The one, most confused at that moment was simply Scarlet, who had no idea what was going on with her mother.

"Mom, what are you doing?" Scarlet's question came out muffled as her mother hugged her ruthlessly, with love.

"So, this is why you came back unannounced." Laura stated as she broke off the hug and looked at her daughter with love and pity...?

"Mom, I don't know what you heard but I can explain-"

"No, you don't need to explain. I already heard you two. This Stewart guy broke your heart, didn't he?" Lauren was the one that coughed uncontrollably and broke the moment of the mother and daughter.

"No, mom-"

"And this is the woman that is the reason why." Laura glared at Lauren making the blonde uncomfortable. Scarlet would've laughed at the situation but she couldn't.

"Mom!" Laura turned towards her daughter as Vanessa walked out of the house, grabbing the three's attention.

"Who wouldn't cheat on her? Look at her clothes. He must have felt like sleeping with a man." Vanessa laughed as Lauren glanced at Scarlet.

'I think she looks cute in the clothes she wears.' Lauren thought as she bit her lower lip.

"Vanessa!" Laura exclaimed at her oldest daughter, who just gave her mother a grin before going back inside the house while still talking to Kevin on her phone.

"Mom, you've got it wrong." Scarlet spoke making both Lauren and Laura to look at her. "She's Stewart's sister and, he and I are-"

"Sister?" Laura spoke again, interrupting Scarlet who just raised her hands in defeat.

"Forget it." She walked rudely inside the house leaving Lauren with Laura.

Lauren smiled a small smile at Laura as she took in the tense situation she was in now.

It had only been two hours since Lauren had come to Scarlet's family house, and Scarlet's uncles and aunts had arrived with their children, making the house louder than before.

Scarlet was in Vanessa's room with her head buried under a pillow as she was wrapped in a blanket, crying her eyes out silently. Lauren sat between Vanessa and Laura as the whole family was gathered in the living room except for Scarlet.

Everyone was busy in a conversation with each other as Lauren sat silent, too overwhelmed by everything.

"So, you're the sister of the guy that cheated on Scarlet?" A guy spoke to Lauren as she smiled tight lipped at him, which only made him more curious.

"Are you single?" He asked as Laura stood up to go somewhere and he quickly occupied the place, beside her.

"Yes."

"Sweet. We can totally hook up." He gave her the best charming smile that he could muster but it didn't work as she compared his smile with Scarlet's.

"No."

"Come on, babe. No one will know." He whispered in her ear which made her move away from him immediately.

"Stay away from Aunty Scar's friend, 'Black'." Out of nowhere, Gregory jumped in between Lauren and the guy that was flirting with her, making him groan.

"Greg, dude. I'm scoring here." The guy whined childishly which made Lauren roll her eyes.

"No, Aunty Scar told me to make you stay away from her friend." The boy spoke as he pushed the guy away with his hands, making the guy wink at Lauren before going away.

Lauren was smiling widely from knowing that Scarlet had told Gregory to keep that guy away from her. She couldn't help but to smile more brightly when she saw the woman walking towards her wearing an over sized hoodie and jeans with a pair of sunglasses.

"Honey, its dark outside already, you don't need sunglasses." Andrew, Mr. Payne, who had introduced himself to Lauren, spoke up as he looked at his daughter with concern.

"Yeah, I know." Scarlet replied without looking at him, with a certain raspiness in her voice that didn't go unnoticed by the blonde girl.

"Come on." She spoke to Lauren as she began to walk towards the front door. Lauren smiled politely at Gregory and the other family members before following the black headed girl.

"Where are we going?" Lauren asked hesitantly as Scarlet closed the front door behind her.

"For a walk." Scarlet gave a simple response as she began to walk towards the street that was now lit up by the street lights.

The silence was deafening as they both walked without uttering a single word, well Lauren wanted to ask a lot of questions but she couldn't because she was afraid of the girl right now.

"Why did he send you here, to laugh at my misery?" Scarlet spoke, breaking the silence as she kept her eyes straight ahead.

"No. He was ashamed of what he did." Lauren spoke quietly as she looked beside her, at the girl.

"Yeah, right. He was in that damn bed with her looking all cocky and you say he felt ashamed, bullshit." Scarlet angrily spat as Lauren flinched away.

"He d-didn't send me." Lauren didn't know why she lied but when Scarlet looked at her, through the sunglasses, she knew why. "I was worried about you."

"W-What?"

"I wanted to comfort you, because I thought that we were friends- are friends -."

Scarlet had stopped walking as she now had all her attention at the blonde. Lauren feeling brave enough, raised her hand and took a hold of Scarlet's sunglasses before taking them off, revealing the red eyes of the girl.

"I'm here now." She wrapped her arms around Scarlet's shoulders before embracing her with a sigh. "I won't hurt you."

Scarlet didn't know what was happening but her heart knew, she was being comforted and it felt a little better knowing that someone had her in their arms instead of having someone in her arms. Her tears came back as she wrapped her own arms around Lauren's back and pulled her impossibly close.

Lauren's breath hitched before she felt her heart speed up from the closeness of their bodies.

Wasn't it ironic, one was finding comfort in the other's arms while the other was finding some kind of love.

Chapter 3

When Lauren woke up the next morning, she expected the house to be as loud as it was last night but she was only greeted with silence. Confused, she got out of the bed she was sharing with Vanessa, while Scarlet lay on a movable mattress on the floor.

She yawned as she stretched her hands, and looked at Scarlet sleep.

'She looks so cute.' She thought to herself with a smile as the said girl tossed and turned before settling down in a comfortable position, snoring away.

She looked at the girl a last time before walking into the walk in bathroom, to make herself a bit presentable.

Last night was a whirlwind of emotions as Lauren had hugged Scarlet close to her as Scarlet cried her eyes out. Lauren was also a bit ashamed of lying to her but she was also happy that it all worked out.

Scarlet had opened up to her and she was willing to let her stay for as long as she wanted, and Lauren mentally planned to stay till the other girl did.

After showering and brushing her teeth, she made her way back into the room where she saw an awake Scarlet. Vanessa was awake as well and yawning with her hands outstretched.

"You look like a cat." Scarlet commented as she threw a pillow at her older sister, who was caught off guard as the pillow hit her in the face.

"Oh, you are so dead." Vanessa threatened as she grabbed the same pillow to throw it at her little sister. "Ha, in your dreams, short stuff."

Lauren knew that she was completely ignored by the two siblings but she didn't care as the two threw pillows at each other, she was happy to see Scarlet a little happier than last night.

Lauren had been introduced to Scarlet's family as she was going to be staying at their house for a while. She met Scarlet's father, mother, her older sister, and her little cousin, Gregory. The rest of the family was not officially introduced to the girl as she had gone out to take that walk with Scarlet.

She blushed as she remembered last night, the way they were so close to each other. Her face was completely heating up while still remembering the moment they shared, when Vanessa noticed the red faced girl standing in the doorway of the bathroom.

"Why is she so red?" Scarlet was about to throw a pillow back at her sister when she turned to look at where Vanessa was pointing.

Scarlet stood up quickly as she went towards Lauren, "Are you okay?" Scarlet shook Lauren out of her reverie, giving her a worried look as Lauren came back to her surroundings.

"What?"

"Are you okay? You're so red." Scarlet looked at Lauren with her eyebrow raised in curiosity. "I was just um remembering something."

Lauren looked away from Scarlet and went towards her bag to get a pair of shoes out. Vanessa and Scarlet glanced at each other before shrugging and fighting to go to the bathroom first.

The Payne household, in the morning was like a lion's den as everyone had a bad temper especially, granny Payne.

Lauren hadn't met granny Payne yet and as she saw the old woman nag to her oldest son, Scarlet's father, she concluded that it wasn't a good time to introduce herself.

The whole house felt like it was invaded by zombies as everyone walked slow and talked like little kids with head nods and gestures. Lauren smiled when she saw Scarlet as fresh as a daisy, playing with Gregory, in the back yard.

She terribly wanted to go to the girl but she was just too embarrassed about last night as well as this morning.

'How many more times am I going to embarrass myself in front of her?' She thought to herself as she stirred her coffee looking out the glass door leading to the backyard, longingly.

"Is there something wrong with your coffee?" Lauren jumped as she looked behind at who had scared her.

"N-No." She mentally face-palmed herself for stuttering in front of the old woman.

"Do you want to go outside?" Granny Payne asked as she sat beside the blonde girl on the chair, with her poodle named Pudding.

Lauren glanced at the poodle before shaking her head, "I was just looking at Gregory play with Scarlet."

"Please, just call her Scar. It suits her better since she scarred everyone's life by being born." Lauren opened her mouth, shocked at the words that she just heard from the old woman.

"Mother!" Lauren's eyes fell on Andrew, Scarlet's father, as he stared his mother down with a glare. Granny Payne shrugged innocently like a child as if she hadn't just said something offending about her own granddaughter.

"It's the truth." She spoke looking straight into Andrew's eyes.

"That's enough. Not in front of Scarlet's friend." Andrew boomed as half of the family came into the kitchen hearing the loud voice.

She gave her son a hard glare before walking out of the kitchen followed by her poodle. "I'm sorry, Lauren. She's just like this with Scarlet." Andrew sighed as he smiled a tired smile at the blonde.

"Why is she like that?" Lauren asked quietly, not wanting to be nosy but couldn't help it.

"That's a story that only she can tell you." A man spoke as Lauren and Andrew looked towards him. The man smiled at Lauren before introducing himself, "I'm Jared. Second brother of Andrew." Lauren shook the out stretched hand and smiled at the man with her best smile.

"She's always like this with Scarlet but she loves Vanessa." Jared spoke as he looked to the back yard at Scarlet playing with his youngest son.

"You don't.... seem to be too close to Scarlet." Jared spoke cautiously as Lauren nodded her head not being offended. "Honestly, we've never spoken more than two words to each other before." Jared and Andrew nodded understandingly.

"Don't worry, we have a whole month together." Jared spoke and Andrew laughed as Lauren looked outside at Scarlet laying on the grass with Gregory bouncing around Scarlet with a happy smile.

Scarlet had no idea why she was in this mess in the first place as she looked outside the huge store window, at the passing people. She didn't know how she agreed to this without getting anything in return except for boredom and sometimes sarcasm from her grandmother.

"This one looks so beautiful on me." Vanessa gushed at herself as she twirled in front of the mirror in the shop.

"Ugh, Vanessa. For the last time, you need a dress for your wedding, not your funeral." Scarlet spoke up getting nasty glares from Vanessa but a nastier one from her grandmother.

"Don't mind her, she's just jealous that she can't rock this dress." Granny Payne spoke soothing words to Vanessa making Scarlet roll her eyes, while Lauren was in her own world as she looked at a white backless wedding dress.

"Mother, please. Scarlet is right. Vanessa needs to pick out a dress for her wedding, a white dress would be better." Laura spoke as she guided her oldest daughter towards the white dresses rack.

Scarlet turned her attention to Lauren, who was busy looking at the same backless dress with a red face as scenarios were starting to come to her mind. She imagined herself wearing the dress and Scarlet dressed in a suit.

"Lauren." Scarlet walked over to the blonde girl, to see her fixated on a dress.

"Yoohoo, Lauren." Scarlet waved her hand in front of Lauren's face, making Lauren come out of her dreamland with a blush on her cheeks.

'I seriously need to stop doing that.' Lauren thought as she mentally face-palmed and physically smiled at Scarlet, making the other girl raise an eyebrow in confusion.

"Do you like this dress?" She asked as she took the dress out of the rack and held it in front of Lauren to see.

"Y-Yeah." Lauren stuttered and Scarlet smiled at her before grabbing her arm and taking her to one of the dressing rooms.

"Go try it on." Scarlet lightly nudged the girl in the dressing room but Lauren shook her head, "It's not my wedding, Scarlet."

"Scar, and that doesn't mean that you can't even try it on." Lauren blushed as she began to speak.

"S-Scar, I don't want to try it on." Scarlet smiled as Lauren spoke her name with such cuteness before she shook her head not taking 'no' for an answer.

"I want to see you in this fucking dress, now go." Scarlet gently pushed the blonde into the dressing room before closing the door, leaving Lauren with a dress, a blush and a thought that didn't do anything better to stop her heart from beating this fast.

'She looks so hot while cursing.'

The moment when Lauren came out of the dressing room with reluctance, was the moment Vanessa felt like a hobo as she saw Lauren 'rocking' a beautiful white backless wedding dress.

"Wow, you look... amazing." Laura was the one that complimented the blonde first as she smiled at her.

"Yeah, you are totally rocking that dress." Jared's wife, Wanda, spoke, who was also invited to the dress picking.

"Eh, she looks okay." Granny Payne spoke as she scrunched up her face in dislike while Vanessa just went back to the dressing room quietly to probably cry.

Lauren smiled at everyone before she looked at Scarlet who had her mouth open wide. Scarlet composed herself before she walked closer to the blonde.

"You are so buying that dress." It wasn't a command or an order but it was more like a request that made Lauren bow her head down before nodding her answer.

"Now go change, before Vanessa starts to feel self conscious and we get uninvited from her wedding." Scarlet joked but Lauren made a look of horror that made the black headed girl laugh.

"I'm just joking, Laur." She spoke and Lauren instantly blushed from the use of her nickname. Only her family called her 'Laur' but when she heard it from Scarlet's mouth, she smiled as it did sound better coming from her mouth.

With a smile playing on her lips, she turned to go back inside the dressing room and change back to her jeans and top.

As she began to unzip the dress from the side, she felt like it was stuck. She raised her arm a little bit higher and tried to unzip it, but it was definitely stuck. She felt so embarrassed as she tried a million times to unzip it but it didn't even move.

"Um, Scar." She spoke a little loud as she didn't want the whole store to know that her zip was stuck.

Scarlet, who was standing just outside the door, quickly responded, "Yeah."

"I think, the zip is stuck." She spoke as a blush crept up her face again.

"Do you want help?" Scarlet asked and Lauren rolled her eyes at the obliviousness of the girl.

"No, I want a latte. Of course, I want help." Scarlet chuckled as she opened the dressing room door just enough to get in. When she went in, she saw Lauren with her head down trying to unzip the thing but it didn't even budge.

"Okay, stop fighting with the damn dress." Lauren jumped a little as she didn't expect Scarlet to be in there so quickly. Lauren stopped her actions and stood still as Scarlet came closer to her. She was immediately reminded of the other night when they both were so close to each other.

Her heart began to speed up as Scarlet lightly lifted the blonde's left hand up so that she could see the zip that denied to go down.

Scarlet concentrated on the zip as she knitted her eyebrows together and brought her tongue out of her mouth. Lauren gushed at the sight as she stared at the black headed girl.

"There." Scarlet spoke as the zip went down and the dress sagged but Lauren quickly grabbed it before it completely came off, with a blush.

"I used to do this with Katie so I know how these type of dresses are." Scarlet spoke unconsciously as she smiled at Lauren, but Lauren didn't give a smile in return. Her heart ached when she heard Scarlet talk about Katie.

"She always managed to get stuck in a dress and then she'd call for help." Scarlet suddenly realized what she had just said and a certain sadness invaded her eyes as she was again reminded of her broken heart.

Lauren smiled sadly at Scarlet, who just shook her head and went out of the dressing room quickly.

Laura had seen her youngest daughter getting out of the dressing room quickly and then going directly out of the store. She raised an eyebrow in confusion, when Lauren quickly got out of the dressing room in panic.

That moment, Laura knew something was being hid from her and she wanted to know what it was.

Chapter 4

Lauren had come back home with the other women of the Payne household and Scarlet had yet to come back to her house and all her family members were worried, well except for granny Payne, who was busy patting Pudding. Lauren was the most worried since she knew just why Scarlet had ran away from the shopping mall in the first place.

"I'm hungry." Granny Payne spoke getting the attention of everyone in the living room.

"Scarlet hasn't come back home yet and you're hungry." Andrew spoke while rubbing his forehead in stress. "Please, if you can't worry about Scarlet at least show some respect."

Granny Payne rolled her eyes before slumping in her chair going back to patting the poodle's head.

Lauren stared at her phone, sending another text to Scarlet. Since Scarlet wasn't picking up Lauren's phone calls, Lauren began to text the said girl.

"What if something happened to her?" Laura spoke with her voice shaky and her expression was evidence of her worry. Vanessa soothed her mother by patting her back, "Scar is a brave and strong girl. Nothing bad is gonna happen, okay?"

Laura nodded her head before looking at her lap with her eyes getting teary. Gregory was sitting in his mother, Wanda's, lap with tears already staining his cheeks.

A click was heard and everyone's attention turned towards the entrance of the living room. Scarlet came in with her eyes covered with sunglasses and her hood was over her head. She stared around the room and her eyes lingered longer on a certain blonde before she was tackled to the floor by none other than Gregory.

"Where were yu, Aunty Scar?" He cried as she patted his head with a sigh. She had been in a bar drowning in tears and cheap cola. Since Scarlet wasn't a drinker, cola was the closest beverage to alcohol for her.

"I'm sorry I made you worry." Her voice was cracked and raspy as she spoke looking towards everyone in the living room. Everyone muttered something before going to the dining room. Laura and Lauren stayed behind as well as Andrew, who was glaring at his daughter.

Scarlet sighed and stood up with Gregory still clinging to her. "Hey Greg, why don't you go to your mom?" Gregory shook his head making Scarlet sigh out before she placed herself on her knees to look at the six year old better.

"I won't go anywhere now, okay?" Gregory looked into Scarlet's eyes for a minute before he nodded hesitantly, leaving her to go to the dining room, while still looking back at the 24 year old.

When Gregory was gone, all hell broke loose as Laura bombarded her daughter with questions and Andrew just stood there nodding his head at every question his wife asked. Lauren stood silently, looking at the three with her own eyes getting teary.

"You, young lady, are so in trouble. You had us worried." Laura spoke while pointing her index finger at her daughter with anger and worry, but mostly anger.

"What she said." Andrew spoke while pointing at his wife.

Scarlet smiled at her parents and nodded frantically. Laura puffed air into her cheeks before walking out of the living room with her feet stomping with every step but stopped at the entrance.

"And come for dinner, now." Scarlet laughed at her mother, who had now left the living room followed closely by her husband. Scarlet was now turned towards Lauren, who was standing there with her watery eyes. Lauren smiled at Scarlet, who without a word spoken, turned around and walked away from her.

Lauren knew that Scarlet was going to probably ignore her now.

After an hour of trying to get Scarlet's attention, Lauren fell on the bed with a long sigh. She was tired of getting the same answer over and over again whenever she tried to talk to Scarlet. "I'm sorry, I'm busy. Can we talk later?" And that later was never going to come by because Lauren knew perfectly well what Scarlet was doing. She was ignoring the matter completely and in other words, she was running away. Yet again.

"You look bummed." Lauren looked up to see Laura standing in the doorway with a coffee in hand and a smirk on her face. "Y-yeah, maybe I'm just homesick." One thing Lauren had noticed since coming back from that shopping trip was that Laura had started giving her these weird looks and smirks all night.

Just like every other night, the Payne household was bustling with games and beverages of all types. Everyone was having the time of their lives, well except for Lauren and Scarlet, who was busy smoking on the roof of the house, without anyone knowing.

"Well, it has been three days since you came here." Laura pointed out and Lauren laughed awkwardly.

"So..."

"I know that you and Scar are hiding something from me." All the color went away from Lauren's face when Laura spoke and all types of bad scenarios played in Lauren's mind in repeat.

'What if she knows about Scarlet being gay? What if she found out that I came here to take her back? What if she found out that I'm attracted to Scarlet in a more than friends way? Wait what?'

Lauren brought herself back to reality where Laura was now beside her quietly sipping her coffee.

"W-what?" Was the unintelligent reply of Lauren as she stuttered while looking all around the room. Praying internally that someone calls Laura and then she would have to go.

"I know that You and Scarlet are hiding something from me." Laura repeated as she stared at Lauren with an eye brow raised in amusement. "You're really red."

Lauren quickly brought her hand to her face. "I-I am?" Laura chuckled before she placed her hand on Lauren's knee. "Don't worry. I'm not gonna drill you with questions."

Lauren nodded dumbly as she smiled lightly at the older woman. "I know how Scarlet is, she's stubborn." The younger blonde woman had no idea where this conservation was going so she just silently listened, nodding occasionally.

"She's not going to forgive that Stewart fella just yet." Lauren's eyes suddenly widened as she understood what was happening here. "Oh. You're talking about that." Lauren sighed in relief making Laura stare at the girl in confusion.

"What else did you think?" Lauren just shook her head at Laura making the older woman more confused. "I'm confused." Lauren chuckled before she stood up from the bed not wanting to make the woman suspicious.

"Can you introduce me to all the others?" Laura stayed confused for a moment but her eyes immediately lit up when Lauren mentioned introductions. "Yeah, let's do that."

Lauren smiled and when Laura got up from the bed and walked out of the room while gesturing Lauren to follow, she sighed another breath of relief. "Thank god she doesn't suspect anything."

The blonde followed the older woman out of the room with another sigh of relief as she thought of what Scarlet would have been doing at the moment.

Lauren had just stepped foot into the living room when she was hit by a sofa cushion.

"Vanessa! Edward hit Scar's pretty friend in the face with the sofa cushion!"

"I did not!"

The blonde woman stood looking at the two twins who were bickering at each other, while Greg was laughing at both of them not from afar.

"Behave, Ed and Ed!" Vanessa's voice was heard from the kitchen and both the twins stopped before glaring at each other. Blake was also sitting in the living room but he was quite busy with his phone to study what was going on around him.

"Black, where's Scar?" Greg asked as he came over to the said man wearing a cute pout. Blake looked up from his phone to glare at the small boy, "For the millionth time, it's Blake."

At the entrance of the living room, Laura and Lauren stood staring at the twins. "Okay, Ed and Ed, come here. Meet Scar's friend, Lauren." Both of the twins looked at Lauren before walking over to her with quick steps.

"Hi, I'm Edmund. I'm the charming and funny one." A hand was stretched out in front of Lauren to shake but before she could take it, Edmund was pushed away by his twin.

"He's totally lying. I'm the charming and funny one, he's just the nerd." The other Ed pushed out his hand while giving a cheeky smile which Lauren found really adorable. "Edward at your service." When Lauren shook his hand, he pecked the back of it like a true gentleman, while his twin brother scoffed from behind him.

"Don't worry. I think both of you are charming and funny." Lauren complimented as she glanced from Edmund to Edward with a sweet smile on her face making the two boys give her a toothy smile back.

"And that's Blake." Laura pointed at the man that sat on the sofa with his eyes trained on his phone. "Mom!" Vanessa's voice was heard from the kitchen making Laura yell back at her. "Yeah?"

"Kevin's gonna be early, so you better make the kids behave!" Vanessa demanded which got her a loud 'Hey!' from the said kids also known as; Greg, Edmund and Edward. "We always behave!"

"No, you don't! And can someone please go find my crazy sister!"

"Aunt Scar ish not crazy! You people are!" Greg shouted as he ran out of the living room to maybe go find Scarlet. Edmund and Edward followed closely behind him while bickering about something.

"We love each other so much here." Laura spoke sarcastically as she smiled at Lauren, who giggled adorably. "Do you have a boyfriend, dear?" Laura interjected making Lauren widen her eyes.

"What?" Lauren choked on her own saliva as she looked at Laura with questioning and confused eyes. "That was a turn of subject."

"Well, do you?" Laura urged as she gestured for the both of them to sit down at the couch that was vacant.

"Um, no."

"Oh, that is such a shame. You're a beautiful young lady. I'm sure men throw themselves at you." Laura remarked as Lauren blushed bashfully.

"No. It's nothing like that." Lauren denied as she sat awkwardly, trying to get the topic off of her. "Maybe you don't notice." Laura shrugged and Lauren just smiled awkwardly.

"I should go find Scarlet. Besides I do need to talk to her about something." Lauren admitted as she stood up quickly getting a confused look from Laura. "I'll be back after I talk to her. Promise." And with that she was out of the living room as fast as possible.

Looking around the house, Lauren had finally found Scarlet sitting on the rooftop of the house with an unlit cigarette between her lips.

"Oh my god, everyone has been looking for you. Well, only the kids but everyone has been wondering where you are." Lauren ranted as she walked carefully towards the sitting girl.

Just as Lauren sat down, Scarlet threw away the unlit cigarette before going to get up. Lauren sighed before she grabbed Scarlet by the arm and bringing her back down to sit beside her.

"We have to talk, and we will talk." Lauren announced as she glared at Scarlet, who was already returning the glare. "Later. We'll talk later."

"This 'later' won't come. So, we're gonna talk now." Lauren demanded as she stared Scarlet down, which made the girl sit down without another word.

"So you miss Katie. What's the big deal?" Lauren started as she took a hold of Scarlet's hand which was clutching harshly at her jeans. "You love her, and she betrayed you. It's going to take time to move on from that." Lauren continued as she brought Scarlet's hand to her own lap.

"That's why I'm here. That's why we all are here, and I'm talking about your family. They don't know about it but they will help you even when you don't want it. We will help you move on." Lauren explained as she smiled at a now frowning Scarlet, who was looking at Lauren in a new light.

"I wish she had just talked to me." A sob escaped Scarlet's lips as she quickly went to wipe at her eyes. "I still wish that she would've just talked to me instead of breaking my trust like that." Lauren watched as Scarlet tried to wipe away her now falling tears.

"And you know what the most pathetic thing about this all is?" Scarlet looked Lauren in the eyes as she smiled painfully.

"That I still want her back. I still want to hold her and tell her how much I am in love with her. I still want her. I still want her." Scarlet broke down as tears came streaming down her cheeks. Lauren watched Scarlet with a pained expression before she wrapped her arms around Scarlet's shoulders tightly.

"That's not pathetic. That's love." And Scarlet cried in Lauren's arms as Lauren looked out into the night sky, as she tried not to tear up herself.

Chapter 5

"**B**aby!" Vanessa screamed just as Kevin entered through the door, making most of the people around her flinch. "Nessa!" Kevin exclaimed back as he took the woman in his arms with a wide smile on his face.

"Yuck, too much gushy gushy." Scarlet mumbled from beside Lauren, who giggled cutely making Scarlet smile at the sound.

Scarlet and Lauren had come back down after a whole half an hour of crying and consoling. Lauren had brightened up Scarlet's mood and now they both were surrounded by the Payne family members.

Lauren had been introduced to some more of the family members like the second brother of Andrew Payne -Scarlet's father- Tyler, and his wife Judith. Their daughter Juliet had also been introduced to the blonde woman, who was excited to know that someone like her had been in the family, a lover of fashion.

Juliet and Lauren had quickly been acquainted and were already becoming best friends.

"I missed you so much. California is so lonely without you there." Kevin admitted as he pecked Vanessa's lips lovingly causing the said woman to giggle like a high school girl.

"Okay, that does it." Scarlet mumbled before going over to the couple to break them apart. "Hi, I'm Scarlet. Vanessa's sister." Scarlet stretched out a hand for Kevin to shake.

Kevin pouted just like Vanessa before he sulkily shook Scarlet's hand. "I'm Kevin."

"So I've heard." Scarlet gave the man a stare that spoke more than words. Kevin shuddered before he took his hand back and smiled nervously.

"Damn it, Scarlet. Don't scare him. Dad already does that." Vanessa complained from behind Scarlet as the said girl laughed before giving Kevin the stare.

"We need to have a long and uninterrupted talk, bub." Vanessa groaned before pushing Scarlet away by her shoulders, before clinging to Kevin like a koala. "I'm serious." Scarlet smirked when Kevin gave her a nod awkwardly.

"Come on, that's enough scaring for now." Lauren dragged Scarlet away by the arm as she walked in the living room where Juliet and Blake sat chatting animatedly about episodes of Grey's Anatomy.

Kevin and Vanessa went to the kitchen where all the elders were, while the living room was the hot spot for the younger people.

Greg was sat watching Ed and Ed play scrabble while drinking juice boxes. "What? He needs to have a talk with me." Scarlet defended as she looked at Lauren, who was giving her the look that said 'leave them be'.

"Come on kids, bed time!" Came the voice of Wanda Payne as she walked into the living room with three glasses of milk.

"Greg, Ed and Ed. Drink up and go to bed." Aunt Wanda handed the glasses of milk to the three children getting whines of denial from them. "A little help please, Scar." Scarlet just stared at the three.

As if on cue, the three kids drank up their glasses of milk quickly before slamming the glasses back on to the tray. "There, all done."

"Bed time, now." Scarlet pointed to the stairs and the three children groaned before walking to the stairs with frowns. Scarlet kissed all of their foreheads making them smile before they said their 'goodnights' and disappeared up the stairs.

Lauren stood admiring the woman with a smile on her face. "Thanks, Scar. They only seem to listen to you." Wanda complimented Scarlet and she just waved it off.

"She's like a children whisperer." Blake spoke up from the sofa as Juliet nodded her head in agreement. "Greg doesn't even say my name right." Blake complained as a pout came on to his face. Scarlet and Lauren laughed while Wanda patted his shoulder before leaving the four young adults in the living room.

"Because you don't play with him." Scarlet pointed out as she went to sit down on the recliner while Lauren sat down beside Juliet.

"The twins love you more than me too." Juliet complained as well as she pouted cutely making Scarlet smile at her. "They can't. You're their big sister." Scarlet spoke making Juliet smile.

"What about me? No comforting words for me." Blake brought the attention of the three women on him. "No. I heard you were flirting with Lauren the day she came here." Scarlet squinted her eyes at him, which made him uncomfortable.

"Uh, who told you that?"

"Oh my god, he flirted with you?" Juliet questioned Lauren, who was busy blushing bashfully. "I have my sources." Scarlet answered Blake, who's eyes widened in realization. "It was Greg, wasn't it? I'm gonna-"

Scarlet arched an eyebrow at his direction making him stop mid-sentence. Juliet and Lauren were now in their own conversation as their attention went away from the flirting to shoes and clothes.

"I'm sorry." He bowed his head in embarrassment making Scarlet sigh.

"It's okay since Lauren didn't mind it that much."

"Scarlet!" Vanessa's voice came from the kitchen before the woman showed herself in the entrance of the living room. "I'll be staying with Kevin in the hotel for tonight."

"Ooh." Blake and Juliet cooed as Vanessa glared at them. "So?" Came Scarlet's question.

"So. Go to bed." Vanessa ordered before she got her jacket from off the coat hanger. Kevin walked to her with his jacket already in his hands as he smiled at Blake and Scarlet.

"No sex." Scarlet warned out of nowhere and Kevin choked on his own saliva, while Vanessa showed her sister the finger. Scarlet laughed before Vanessa and Kevin said their farewell, walking out of the front door.

"Well, time for sleep." Scarlet spoke before getting up off the recliner. "Yeah." Blake followed after.

Juliet and Lauren were still in the middle of conversing so Scarlet just left after saying 'goodnight'.

Walking into the room, the first thing that Lauren saw was that the extra mattress was gone. The second thing she had noticed was that Scarlet was already asleep to even answer the many questions of Lauren.

"Where am I gonna sleep?" She mumbled to herself as she began to pace around the room. Looking at Scarlet, she just wanted to coo at the cuteness but she refrained herself from doing such a thing.

Juliet and Lauren had talked till they felt tired and then they talked some more before they both retired to their sleeping rooms.

"I should just go change into my pajamas before I go find a place to sleep." She mumbled to herself again and then nodded her head in agreement before she went into the bathroom, closing the door with a light click.

It was a little noise but it was noise nonetheless and it was what woke up a sleeping Scarlet from her slumber.

"Lauren?" She rubbed at her eyes as she groggily called out to the blonde that was in the bathroom. Lauren, who was busy changing into a long shirt, called back, "Yeah?"

"Okay." Scarlet nodded her head before she laid back down on the bed with a subtle plop.

After Lauren had fully changed into her pajama shorts and long t-shirt, she walked out into the bed room where Scarlet lay awake waiting for her.

"Um, where's the mattress?" She asked Scarlet just as she saw that the other woman was awake. "Oh, yeah. Uncle Tyler needed it. You can sleep with me tonight." The nonchalant tone of Scarlet's voice was what made Lauren blush profusely.

"Uh, what? With you?" Lauren questioned and Scarlet only nodded in response as her eyes had begun to close. "Yeah, with me. In here. This bed is large enough for the both of us."

Lauren nodded her head before she got in the bed beside a sleepy Scarlet. "Could you close the light too?" Scarlet asked groggily as she yawned.

"Mmhmm." Lauren closed the lights as she laid down beside Scarlet with a pounding heart and a blushing face.

Scarlet turned to her side and Lauren's face flushed more than it did before. The only thoughts swirling in her head was the fact that Scarlet was there beside her, only an arm's distance away.

After a lot of overthinking, Lauren finally found a result to her situation as she placed a pillow in between their bodies and then sighed in relief.

Closing her eyes to sleep, Lauren could still feel the pounding of her heart in her ears while she tried to slow it down.

Waking up in the Payne household was a dreaded thing. No one wanted to wake up in the morning and considering that Scarlet was technically not used to waking up late in the morning, she was the first one to wake up.

And the moment her eyes opened, she saw blonde hair, lots of blonde hair. On further inspection she found out that her body was tangled up with Lauren's body, with their legs tangled together and Lauren's arms wrapped around her waist while Lauren's head rested on Scarlet's chest.

Scarlet tried to wiggle out of Lauren's hold but the blonde woman just tightened her hold on Scarlet's body as if she didn't want her to leave. Scarlet sighed before she weighed the pros and cons of staying in bed till late in the morning.

She'd miss her run, but she'd not be sweaty. She'd have a few more hours of good sleep with a human sized pillow cuddling up to her, but then she'd become out of shape.

After a lot of thought, sleep had won the argument and Scarlet had decided to wrap her arms around Lauren's body as well and snuggle closer to her before falling asleep again.

An hour later, the person to wake up next was Lauren, who had a sudden urge to pee. She woke up to the smell of lavender which she liked just from the first sniff and decided to sniff some more.

After smelling the lavender scent, she realized that she had arms wrapped around her body and she was laying on an oddly moving pillow.

Moving her hand around, she had found out the hard way that the oddly moving pillow was none other than Scarlet. Jumping away from Scarlet, their body broke apart and Scarlet jolted up as if she had just been attacked.

Lauren blushed as Scarlet's eyes settled on her. "What happened?" Scarlet asked while she scratched her head before she looked up to the wall to see the clock just about to strike 9.

"I had to pee." Lauren admitted embarrassingly as she looked away from Scarlet's gaze. "Okay."

Scarlet laid back down with a sigh as Lauren got up off the bed to go to the bathroom. "Be back quick, you are really nice at cuddling." Lauren stopped just outside the bathroom door as her face heated up and she almost choked on her own spit.

Quickly entering the bathroom door, Lauren leaned against it while trying to control her fast beating heart.

'We cuddled and she's indifferent about the whole situation. I should be too. But why am I not?

A question she didn't have an answer to.

Chapter 6

Walking into the kitchen, Scarlet noticed how her grandmother was standing on her tippy toes looking for something in the upper most cabinet. Scarlet chuckled to herself before she went over to her grandmother and stood beside her.

"What do you need?"

"Nothing that concerns you." Granny Payne scoffed as she kept rumbling in the cabinet while still standing on her toes. "Oh come on, let me help you or you'll break a hip." Another scoff came from Granny Payne as she stepped aside and looked up at Scarlet, due to the said woman's height.

"I need Pudding's can of food. It's in the back." Scarlet nodded before she began to search for the can of dog food while wondering who had put it this far into the cabinet.

Granny Payne looked at Scarlet's back with a look of pain as she remembered something specifically about her husband, who had died just a day after Scarlet's birth.

"Never mind, I don't need it anymore." Granny Payne announced as she turned around to leave the kitchen with quick steps. "I can get it." Scarlet spoke as she turned around to find that her grandmother wasn't behind her anymore.

A sigh escaped her lips as she turned back around to find the can in the cabinet. When she had finally found the can of dog food, she carefully got it out of the cabinet and placed it on top of the kitchen counter.

Looking at the kitchen door, she felt a dull ache in her heart, before she wandered off into the back yard.

It was still early in the morning and most of the Payne family was still asleep while a few were awake.

When Lauren had finally done her business, she had come out of the bathroom to find that Scarlet was wide awake and had her cellphone in her hand. A small part of Lauren was rejoicing at the thought that she didn't have to cuddle with Scarlet again but the other part of her, the fairly large part; was disappointed.

Scarlet had excused herself to go get a cup of coffee while Lauren had gone to the guestroom that consisted of the Payne kids; namely, Blake, Juliet, the twins and Greg.

Just as she entered the room, Lauren was hit with the sounds of snoring and bickering. The snoring was undoubtedly coming from the half-naked Blake, while the three kids were fighting over an action figure.

Juliet sat on a movable mattress, looking at her phone with determination as she typed away quickly.

"How can you stay calm in this chaos?" Lauren asked just as she sat down next to Juliet with a plop.

"When you're related to them, it comes naturally." Juliet joked as she looked up from her phone to stare at Lauren's red face. "What happened to you?"

"What? I'm okay." Juliet raised a perfect eyebrow up at the blonde woman. "Your face is all red." Juliet stated and Lauren's face became much more red as if pointing it out fueled it.

"It's probably nothing." Lauren waved it off as she tried to avoid looking in Juliet's eyes. "Oh my god, do you like Blake?"

"What? Ew, no." Lauren glanced at the shirtless sleeping Blake with disgust as she turned back to look at Juliet. "Then what is it? Is it someone else?" Juliet's eyebrows began to wiggle as she smirked at the blonde woman.

"There is someone." Lauren muttered to herself but Juliet heard it as an excited squeal came out of her mouth, grabbing the kids' attention.

"Is she okay?" Ed loudly asked the other Ed as Greg looked at Juliet with his head tilted to the side. "I can hear you, Edward."

"I'm not Edward, he is." Ed pointed at Edward with a frown making Juliet apologize quickly.

"I'm just kidding, I am Edward."

The resemblance of the two twins always confused people, there family as well and Juliet, who was the sister of the two, couldn't even tell them apart except for the different interests of the two brothers.

"I am going to kill you two if you don't leave right away." Juliet growled as she placed her phone beside her. "Sheesh, woman. Can't even take a joke."

Ed and Ed got up off from their own movable mattress before they went out of the room with Greg, who was awfully quiet.

After the kids had left, Juliet turned back to Lauren, who was trying her best to not blush again. "Tell me all of the details and I mean all."

"It's nothing big, just a little crush." Lauren explained as she stretched out her legs from a bent position. "Doesn't matter. I want details."

Lauren sighed before she began, "Well, she just got out of a relationship-"

"What!?" Lauren flinched from the loudness of Juliet's voice. "She!"

"Oh my god." Lauren muttered as she slapped her forehead, realizing her mistake. Thoughts swirled around her head that now the whole Payne household will know that she has a crush on a female and Juliet won't talk to her, and she'd probably have to leave the house right away. She won't even be invited to the wedding as well.

"Uh, yes. I have a crush on a girl." Lauren admitted as she slumped her shoulders waiting for a negative response from her new friend.

The response that Lauren was waiting for didn't come, instead came squealing noises as Juliet fan girled.

"Is she good looking?" Juliet asked after a whole minute of fan girling, and Lauren staring at her with confusion and surprise. Lauren snapped out of her daze to give a slight nod of agreement, at which Juliet squealed again.

"Okay, you have to stop doing that." Lauren pointed out as she began to feel comfortable with this.

"Sorry. But I'm just so excited." Juliet laughed at herself while Lauren smiled at her. "Thanks for understanding." She thanked shyly and Juliet cooed at the cuteness before she spoke something that Lauren was definitely not expecting.

"Besides, now you can finally talk Scar into coming out as well."

"What?" The shock was evident in Lauren's face as she stared dumbfounded at the red head.

"Scar's also a lesbian." The nonchalance in Juliet's voice was what made Lauren's eyes open wider than they had ever opened before. "You know."

"Of course, I know. I'm her sist-"

"Wait, you knew as well?" Juliet cut herself off as she squinted her eyes at Lauren making Lauren chuckle nervously. "Yes."

"Wait, then are you two a couple or something?" Juliet's voice dropped a little as she leaned closer to Lauren to whisper.

"No. I wish." Lauren face palmed herself immediately just as the words left her lips. "You like her!" Juliet stated loudly and Lauren flinched before she covered Juliet's lips with her hand.

"Could you speak any louder?" Lauren hissed as she turned to look at a still snoring Blake.

"I'm sorry." Juliet apologized just as Lauren took back her hand. "But if you like her and she's into girls, then why aren't you confessing your love your love to each other and riding a unicorn into the sunset?" Lauren laughed at the colorful imagination of the girl.

"First off, it isn't love, it's a mild crush." Lie. "And second off, she already has a girlfriend, or had." Lauren listed off with a little disappointment.

"But what about that Stewart guy?" Juliet asked confusedly as she looked at Lauren for answers.

"It's a long story."

"We seem to have a lot of time." Juliet smirked and Lauren glanced at a sleeping Blake before she broke.

After a few minutes, Juliet was made aware of the whole situation that had happened in New York. Lauren told her everything about how Katie, Scarlet's girlfriend, had cheated on her with Lauren's brother, Stewart, also the boss of Scarlet.

"Oh God, that's is a new level of fucked up."

"Tell me about it." Lauren muttered as she folded her legs up beneath her. "I hate this Katie for breaking my favorite cousin's heart."

"I hate her too." Lauren admitted and then instantly got a smirk from Juliet that spoke volumes. "What are you waiting for then, this is your chance."

"What?"

"You can win Scarlet's heart by confessing your love." Juliet spoke excitedly as Lauren shook her head frantically. "Crush."

"And I'm not going to just fall into her lap just because she's single now. She's heartbroken." Lauren mentioned as she sighed.

Juliet fell back on her back as she groaned loudly. "That sounds a bit sexual." Juliet commented and Lauren fell on her back laughing.

"It does, doesn't it?"

"You can try it."

"I'm starting to think that you're mad." Lauren confessed as she shook her head at her.

"What's there to lose?" Juliet pointed out as Lauren began to wonder.

Scarlet was sitting in the living room drinking a cup of warm chocolate milk just like Greg, who was sitting beside her smiling up at her while drinking the same thing.

"It's good, isn't it?" Greg nodded his head cutely as he sucked at the straw.

Everyone was now awake, even Blake, who was now fully dressed. Vanessa and Kevin had come back from the hotel with all of Kevin's stuff which had brought up a million questions that Vanessa calmly answered.

"He's gonna stay in my room." 'It's my room', thought Scarlet as she scoffed before padding away into the living room.

"Lauren, you and Scar can sleep in the guestroom where Juliet and Blake are staying." Lauren simply nodded as she and Juliet went to the living room as well where Scarlet was sitting with a frown, staring at the t.v that showed cartoons.

"We'll have sleep overs every night till the wedding." Juliet excitedly spoke as she jumped on the sofa beside Scarlet, who just scoffed.

"She'll get over it." Juliet murmured as she took hold of the t.v remote which was in one of the twin's hands.

"Hey!"

"Go out and play. Kids your age shouldn't be watching t.v." Juliet ordered as she glared at her brothers. "Scar." They both ran to Scarlet as she chuckled at them. "She's being mean to us."

"Yeah, like she'll listen to your lies even after seeing everything happen." Juliet laughed at them making the twins pout adorably. "Jules." Scarlet spoke in a tone of warning as she looked at the said girl, making Juliet look at Scarlet in disbelief.

"Whatever." Juliet waved her hand as she left the t.v remote on the sofa before getting up and stomping out of the living room making the twins celebrate.

Scarlet laughed at the girl while Lauren was torn between two things; first was to keep looking at Scarlet laugh like a kid, which was extremely cute in her eyes, or she could go and accompany her new friend.

For a while, Lauren sat glued to the sofa, looking at Scarlet's laugh turn into a smile that lit up the whole living room, but she immediately looked away when Scarlet's eyes turned to her.

"You're red." Lauren immediately brought her hands to her cheeks in embarrassment. "I should go see where Juliet is." Lauren quickly got up off the sofa and walked out of the living room as fast as her legs could take her.

"Oh my god." She muttered to herself just as she got out of the living room.

She was just half way up the stairs when her phone began to ring inside of her jeans pocket. Confusedly, she got her phone out of her pocket and immediately frowned at looking at the screen.

Rejecting the call, she continued up the stairs indifferently as if her brother hadn't just called her.

It wasn't such a surprising thing for her since she had been rejecting all the calls from Stewart since she had come to Scarlet's house.

She didn't want anything to do with Stewart for the time being because everything was going so great with Scarlet and her family. Lauren didn't want to think about her life in New York, specifically her brother.

Besides, it wasn't like his brother would show up at Scarlet's house. He knew about distance and why people wanted it in the first place, and the distance that Scarlet had put in between New York and her wasn't just out of boredom, it was completely serious.

He had to know that he had broken up Scarlet's relationship and on top of that, he had the audacity to even think of himself as the victim.

He was in the wrong and he knew that himself.

The whole family was sitting in the living room, preparing for the wedding, except for Kevin and the older Payne men as well as the children, as they were out in the town to get suits.

The rest of the Payne family was sitting in the living room as Vanessa was picking out the decorations for the wedding.

"Why am I even here?" Blake complained as he sat between Scarlet and Juliet. "You and me both, bud." Scarlet mumbled sourly as she looked at Vanessa pointing excitedly at every decoration that she could see in the brochure.

Vanessa and Laura were sitting on the carpet as Wanda and Judith -Scarlet's aunts-, were busy on their phone talking to caterers about different things.

"Don't be so whiny." Juliet commented as she leaned backwards so that both Scarlet and Blake could hear. Lauren unconsciously nodded her head as she was sitting beside Juliet on the carpet as well while Blake and Scarlet occupied the couch with their legs up.

"But I wanted a suit too." Blake whined while Scarlet nodded her head with a frown as well. "I want a suit too, I hate dresses." Scarlet commented as she leaned back on the sofa with a sigh.

Lauren looked at Scarlet with a small smile on her face, "You look amazing in a suit too."

Three set of eyes turned to Lauren as she sat confused before she saw the smirk on Juliet's face which pretty much said it all. "Did I just...?"

Juliet nodded her head with the smirk still on her face and Lauren had nothing else to do but to blush and hide her face from Blake and Scarlet's eyes. Lauren groaned when she heard the laughter of Blake but she groaned even louder when Scarlet said an awkward 'thanks' to her.

"I'm gonna......" Lauren stood up abruptly while making weird hand gestures before rushing out of the living room as if her life depended on it.

"Where did she go?" Laura asked from across the room as she squinted her eyes at the three young adults. "What did you three do?" She asked after the three remained awfully quiet.

"Nothing! We did nothing." Juliet burst out, as Scarlet and Blake glanced at each other before they looked at Juliet. "I'll go see where she went." Scarlet quickly got off of the couch before she went out of the living room and opted to go up the stairs first.

Walking into the guest room where Scarlet and Lauren were to sleep in for now, she looked at the blonde that sat in a corner with her legs close to her chest, and her head bowed down.

"Are you okay?" Scarlet asked carefully as she walked slowly over to the girl.

"Oh my god, yeah. Yeah." Lauren spoke quickly as she sniffed a little. Scarlet's expression softened as she sat down beside the blonde draping an arm over Lauren's shoulders.

"Were you crying?" Lauren denied to look into Scarlet's eyes as she shook her head, making her hair fall over her face. "Okay. What were you doing then?" Scarlet snuggled closer to Lauren as she brought Lauren's body closer to her own, much to the blonde's pleasure.

"N-Nothing." Lauren stuttered as she tried to wipe away a few stray tears that had fell out of her eyes. "If this is about how you complimented me downstairs, it's okay."

"No, it isn't about that." Lauren spoke in a low voice.

"Then is it about how Blake laughed at you, I could punch him into next week for you." Lauren giggled making Scarlet smile at the sound. "It isn't about that either, and besides, he's a good-looking man. He needs his face." Scarlet gave out a loud laugh as Lauren giggled adorably.

"Don't say that in front of him, the next thing we want is his ego inflating some more." Scarlet joked and Lauren nodded her head with a small smile as she stared at Scarlet.

"Now tell me why you were crying and why you left like that?" Lauren's smile disappeared as she looked into Scarlet's brown eyes.

"You won't get angry. Or ignore me." Lauren spoke as she pointed at the brown eyed girl.

"No, I wouldn't." Scarlet gave a smile for encouragement and Lauren heaved a sigh before she turned her entire beauty towards Scarlet's.

"I have a-"

"Scarlet!" Both Lauren and Scarlet jumped at the loud call of Laura.

"Yeah, mom!" Scarlet yelled back as she showed Lauren her index finger as to say to give her a minute. "There's a gentleman here to meet you!" Laura yelled back and both Lauren and Scarlet looked at each other before they got off the floor to go downstairs to see who this 'gentleman' was.

Descending the stairs with Scarlet, Lauren was cursing at the universe for disturbing her confession.

"Hello, Scarlet." Looking at the man standing in the middle of the living room, Scarlet's first reaction was to rush over to him and punch him in the face brutally as Wanda and Laura, both screamed at her while Vanessa and Judith tried to pull Scarlet away from the man.

Her second reaction to the 'gentleman' was to kick his balls as hard as she could while yelling, "Get out of my damn house!"

And Lauren stood in the doorway of the living room looking horrified at the whole situation. She had an idea why Stewart was here and she wasn't liking it one bit.

Chapter 7

The aftermath of what Scarlet had done wasn't taken lightly from her mother and aunts, who all gave her a good scolding about how fists don't always resolve a problem.

Blake and Juliet were sitting with dopey smiles on their faces as they looked at Stewart's black eye, while mumbling to each other about how good a punch Scarlet threw.

Vanessa stayed indifferent as she squinted her eyes at the man that was sat with an icepack to his left eye, on the recliner.

"You don't just punch someone like that!" Laura yelled at Scarlet, who was sat beside Vanessa on the carpet while she iced her quickly bruising hand, occasionally glaring at Stewart.

"Look at your hand, you just didn't hurt him, you hurt yourself too." Wanda -Juliet's aunt- lectured as she pointed at Scarlet's hand.

Lauren, who had quickly helped her brother up off the ground after Scarlet had punched him, was sitting on the arm rest of the recliner while watching the Payne women grind Scarlet with lecture after lecture.

"Don't tell her family that Katie cheated on her with you. They don't know that Scarlet is gay." Lauren whispered in Stewart's ear, making him look at the blonde in disbelief. "What!?" Stewart whisper yelled as Lauren shrugged. "They also think that you cheated on her."

"I repeat, what!?" Lauren ignored Stewart as she looked at Scarlet's bruising hand with worry evident on her face.

"Just so you know, Scar took kick boxing lessons when she was in high school." Blake came over to warn Stewart as he looked at him with evident fear. "Hasn't she ruined my face enough?" Blake shrugged with a smirk before he went back to sit with Juliet, who gave Stewart a wink.

"Is her whole family like this?" Stewart whispered in Lauren's ear who broke away her stare from Scarlet to look at her brother. "Like what?"

"Dysfunctional." Lauren gave Stewart an unamused stare as she shook her head in disappointment.

"He's the one that started this all!" Scarlet yelled to her mother and aunts as they took a pause in lecturing her. "He should leave right now!"

"But I just want to apologize!" Stewart spoke up from beside Lauren as he stared at Scarlet. "Apologize? Do you even know what that means?!" Scarlet stood up and was gonna approach Stewart with her fists clenched, but she was stopped by Vanessa, who had also stood up and stopped the woman by placing her hands on her shoulders.

"Don't." Vanessa looked into her sister's eyes that were filled with rage. Scarlet looked back into Vanessa's eyes before she backed away. "At least ask him why the hell he is here, anyway?"

"He can't just fly here out of New York to beg me to come back, if he wanted me back, he would have sent someone else in his place." Scarlet spoke as she sat down beside Blake with a glare sent Stewart's way.

"I was here to see Lauren; she wasn't answering my calls." Lauren grabbed Stewart's shoulder as an attempt to make him stop talking. "I sent her here to get you back, but she stopped taking my calls after she came here. I was worried about her."

Lauren internally prepared herself as she looked at Scarlet, who looked back at her with confusion. "But she said that she came here to comfort me, to be there for me."

"Ha-ha, no. I sent her, in return for an ice-cream sundae." Stewart chuckled, not sensing the tense atmosphere that was now filling the living room.

"You're lying!" Scarlet had nothing else to do but to deny the claims as she didn't know for certain if he was lying or not. "No, I'm not lying, ask Lauren." He looked at Lauren, who had her head bowed as she tried to not look at Scarlet's hurt filled eyes.

"But she said…. you said you were here for me!" Scarlet yelled at Lauren as she stood up abruptly while pointing a finger at the blonde's direction.

Stewart shrinked in the recliner when he saw the raw anger in Scarlet's eyes as she tried to take it out without doing anything bad to the blonde that sat with her head down and tears already welling up in her eyes.

"You lied to me." Scarlet didn't know what was worse, the thought that Lauren had lied to her or the thought that she hadn't expected it from her. Not knowing what to do, Scarlet did one thing she knew how to do best. She rushed out of the living room and then out of the house, slamming the front door behind her harshly.

"I think I peed a little." Everyone's eyes that were staring at the doorway of the living room turned to Stewart as he smiled nervously. Juliet and Blake were the ones that burst out laughing like hyenas as they spoke incoherent words in between.

Laura, who looked at Stewart in horror, immediately told the man about the bathroom which was down the hallway. Wanda and Judith looked at each other before they went over to Lauren, who was still in the same position as before.

"It's okay, honey." Wanda spoke up as she stroked Lauren's hair which were falling around her face. Lauren sniffled a little before she quickly embraced the other woman, crying into her chest.

Wanda looked at Judith, who shrugged in response, patted Lauren's back before stroking it.

"What in the name of God is happening here? Can't you let an old lady sleep." Granny Payne barged into the living room with Pudding yipping in her arms. "Great timing, Grandma." Juliet spoke sarcastically as she went over to comfort Lauren as well after her fit of laughter was done.

"Why, what happened?" Granny Payne asked to no one in particular as she looked around the living room in confusion.

"Nothing." Vanessa answered her as she gave Lauren a glance before walking out of the living room to go upstairs. "It's a long story." Blake sighed as he went to get a glass of water for Lauren, as ordered by his mother -Wanda-.

When the Payne men and children had come back from their shopping spree, they tried to murder Stewart after being told the whole story. The kids were more willing to let him live after finding out that he had 'peed a little' in his pants. That was embarrassment enough to make him want to kill himself.

Blake and Juliet were sure to inform everyone about what had happened, leaving no detail out. Lauren was in the guestroom which was shared by the Payne children and she was wrapped up in a blanket, sulking.

There was no sign of Scarlet as she hadn't come home yet and Granny Payne was just as indecent as she was when Scarlet had disappeared the first time.

Pudding was yipping and bouncing around Stewart as if he loathed his presence, which could be the case since everyone in the family was looking at him with hostility except for Granny Payne, who was just seconds away from patting his back as if he had done something good.

Stewart wanted to go and talk to his sister but he was stopped by the two bodyguards who were sitting in a circle just outside of the guestroom with little action figures as soldiers.

Greg and the twins glared at him, until he disappeared out of their sight, before going back to playing with their action figures.

Lauren was bawling her eyes out, thinking how she had lost all of her chances of getting close to Scarlet now, when she felt her phone vibrating on the floor beside her mattress.

Picking it up with nimble fingers, she pressed call before putting it against her ear. "Hey, Katieeeee! How are ya?" Lauren could hear the slur in Scarlet's voice as she quickly sat up, while wiping at her eyes.

"Scarlet, are you...drunk?" It was a question which was asked out of disbelief as Lauren took the phone away from her ear to check the caller id, which undoubtedly said 'Scar'.

"Yeah, who else would it be, babyyy?" Scarlet hiccupped at the end of the sentence as her words slurred more than before. "Where are you?" Lauren asked as she got up off the mattress before straightening out her large t-shirt.

"I'm at a bar, duh." Scarlet giggled adorably but Lauren didn't have the energy to acknowledge it. "Which bar?" Lauren questioned as she put on a pair of shorts before wearing her flats.

Opening the door, she saw the kids playing but they immediately stopped when they saw Lauren. "Are you okay now?" Greg asked cutely as he stood up to look at Lauren. Lauren, who could hear the distinct giggling and slurring of Scarlet, just nodded towards Greg before making her way to the stairs while the kids followed her.

Reaching downstairs, Lauren searched for Stewart who was sat in the kitchen being stared at by the Payne men as they whispered in each other's ears. Even Kevin was glaring at Stewart even though he, himself, was scared of Scarlet.

Lauren found Stewart and quickly went to him. "Did you bring a car?" Knowing Stewart's travelling habits, she knew that he never travelled without bringing a car with him to the place where he was going.

"Yeah, why?" Stewart looked at her with a questioning look as he took out the car keys from inside his new pants pocket, that he had changed into after his little accident.

Lauren snatched the keys once they were out of his pocket before turning away to walk out of the kitchen. "None of your business."

Stewart stared at the retreating back of Lauren as he sighed before slumping in his seat.

"Where is Lauren going?" Juliet asked just as she entered the kitchen followed by Blake. "Yeah." Blake spoke as well.

"I don't know." Stewart spoke as everyone stared at him with questioning looks. "She just took my car keys. She didn't say where she was going."

Driving with one hand while the other clutched her phone tightly against her ear, Lauren knew that she was breaking multiple rules but she didn't care. All she cared about was the fact that Scarlet was hurt so much that she had took to drinking.

Everyone knew how much Scarlet hated drinking and how much she loathed people that drank, and tonight, she was the one that she hated.

Parking at the bar's parking lot, Lauren rushed out of the car without even locking it behind her as she went to the front of the bar.

Entering the shady looking bar, she immediately recognized the black-haired girl who was still holding her phone and drinking.

"Scarlet?" Lauren called out after she had reached her, making Scarlet turn around in her seat with a giggle. "Katie." Scarlet slurred with her half-lidded eyes as she threw her arms around the blonde who was definitely not expecting to get a hug after what she had done. But that's how drinking is.

"Come on, we have to get you home." Lauren spoke softly to Scarlet, who nodded her head as she got up off the bar stool, stumbling occasionally.

"I was waiting for you, ya know." Scarlet spoke as she poked Lauren's nose lightly with a giggle. "Just like how I did outside the school, for you to come out with a smile on your face." Scarlet slurred as she stumbled but Lauren caught her by grabbing her arm tightly.

"I always loved your smile." Lauren tried to ignore the slurs that were coming from the drunk girl but she couldn't because the slurs kept reminding her of how she didn't have a chance with Scarlet.

"Why aren't you speaking to me?" The two had exited the bar and were now in the parking lot where Lauren was leading them to Stewart's car. "Are you mad at me for drinking?" Lauren looked at Scarlet to see that she was on the verge of tears. "I didn't mean to drink, i-it just happened."

"I know." Lauren mumbled as she sighed before bringing Scarlet to the passenger side of the car and opening the door. "I'll drive." Scarlet spoke up as she closed the door and started to wiggle drunkenly to the driver's side of the door. "No, you can't, you're drunk." Lauren grabbed Scarlet's arm and stopped her from moving.

"But you don't know how to drive, Katie." Scarlet slurred as her half-lidded eyes were falling shut but Scarlet forced them to stay open. "It'll be okay, we're gonna go to your parents' house and you can sleep there." Lauren spoke softly just as she saw Scarlet's eyes trying to stay closed.

Scarlet nodded her head and Lauren opened the passenger door again, and this time Scarlet complied as she sat obediently in the passenger seat.

Lauren sighed before she got in the car herself, before buckling up Scarlet, who was now fast asleep with light snores coming out of her slightly open mouth. Lauren could feel tears trying to well up in her eyes as she saw how broken Scarlet looked right now.

And Lauren knew that she was equally responsible for hurting her as well as Katie and Stewart.

Parking the car in the driveway of the house, Lauren got out and went to the other side of the car, to get Scarlet out as well. But since the said girl was asleep, she knew that she needed help from someone. So, she went and rang the doorbell while waiting for the door to open.

It was Blake who had opened the door with a slight frown on his face, but his frown immediately turned upside down when he saw Lauren.

"You're back, I thought you left." Lauren shook her head before she grabbed his hand and brought him to the passenger side of Stewart's car. "Is that Scar?" Blake asked as he studied the way she was asleep. "Yes, she's drunk."

"What?" Blake's eyes automatically found hers as he quickly went to open the door and bring Scarlet out of the car carefully. Scarlet just hummed in her sleep before she snuggled closer to her cousin's chest as he looked at Lauren.

"Don't tell aunt Laura, she's going to throw a fit. I'll sneak her into the house, you just distract everyone." Blake spoke to Lauren, who immediately nodded her head before walking into the house calmly and casually as if nothing had happened.

"Lauren? Where did you go?" Juliet saw the blonde first and opted to question her while taking her to the living room where everyone was. Blake, who had closed the front door slowly behind him with his foot grabbed the opportunity to slip past the attention of his family, to go upstairs with light but quick steps.

Lauren shook her head before answering, "Just needed some fresh air."

"In my car?" Stewart snorted and everyone glared at him for even speaking up. Lauren nodded her head before throwing the car keys towards him. "You should leave right now, Art."

"What? But I just got here today." Stewart protested as he stood up from the recliner with a frown. "I don't care, just leave. You've done enough."

"You are my sister, Lauren. My little sister. I don't take orders from anyone, especially not you." Stewart spoke as he pointed a finger at the blonde, who was only seconds away from slapping him across his face.

"What else do you want to see, Stewart? Isn't this much enough? Isn't breaking her enough?" Lauren sighed out tiredly as she stared at her brother who' eyes softened. "I didn't mean to-"

"I know, but she doesn't know. Just leave, please." Everyone was looking at the exchange of words as Stewart sighed before walking over to Lauren, who was standing at the doorway of the living room.

"You have a lot to explain." Stewart whispered in her ear as he looked back at the Payne family before he walked out of the house, gently shutting the front door behind him.

Lauren quickly rushed out of the room to go upstairs to the guestroom as thoughts of Scarlet swirled around in her head.

She knew that nothing could happen now, because she already had found herself falling for the girl, with the broken heart.

****

A new chapter. Vote if you like and comment what you liked. ;)

Have a great day and smile, oh and also, be kind to people. What you give away comes back to you.

Chapter 8

"Ugh, my head's killing me." Were the first words that left Scarlet's mouth when she woke up. The next words were, "Why are you two staring at me like that?"

Juliet and Blake were sat on their respective mattresses as they stared intently at the black-haired girl. Blake had told Juliet about how Scarlet was undeniably drunk last night, and how the both of them had heard the slurs that were just spewing out of her mouth about the one and only Katie.

"Who's Katie?" Blake opted to ask as he stared at Scarlet, who looked like she had seen a ghost. "How do you know that name?" Juliet and Blake's eyes squinted at Scarlet as she squinted her own back at her cousins.

"We asked you a question first."

"I'm older than you."

"I'm the exact same age as you." Blake retorted as he smirked triumphantly while Scarlet sighed audibly. "She's my.... friend." She spoke as she tried not to make eye contact with her two cousins while holding her throbbing head.

"We heard something truly different about her last night." Juliet spoke with a smirk on her face as she wiggled her eyebrows at Scarlet. "Yeah, something like 'Katie, I loved you!'."

"I did not say anything like that." Scarlet argued as she looked away from her cousins, denying to make any type of eye contact. "Yeah, you did." Blake had a smug look on his face when Scarlet sighed.

"She was my girlfriend." Scarlet emphasized as she rubbed her aching head. "She cheated on me." Blake gasped but Juliet stayed indifferent since she already knew.

"We should hunt that bitch down." Blake practically growled as he pounded his fist on his open palm.

"Woah, woah. Back up. No cursing and definitely no hunting anyone down. And please don't tell anyone else about the fact that I had a girlfriend." Blake nodded his head frantically as Scarlet gave him a look that basically said, 'behave'.

"Now, you answer my questions."

"Okay, what do you want to ask?" Juliet crossed her legs as she leaned back on her hands. "First, why does my head hurt like I slammed it hard on something?" Scarlet asked as she groaned loudly.

"That, my sister, is called a hangover." Blake smirked at the confused look on Scarlet's face. "Boy, you're really ignorant to the things that you don't like."

"It's because of the heavy drinking you did last night." Blake explained slowly as he glanced at Juliet.

"I drank last night." Scarlet's face held horror and recognition as bits and pieces of last night surfaced from the back of her head to the front.

"I drank last night!" She yelled before she looked at her cousins. "Does mom know?"

"No, we got you covered there." Blake waved his hand dismissively as Scarlet looked at him in gratefulness. "You should thank Lauren, she's the one that brought you home last night." Blake added.

"And also apologize to her, you kept calling her Katie." Juliet smirked when Scarlet groaned audibly. "Well, look at the bright side, at least Stewart is gone."

Scarlet looked at her cousins with an eyebrow raised while her cousins shrugged. "Thank Lauren for that too."

"I don't want to talk to her." Scarlet groaned as she got up to clean herself up. Her body smelled distinctly of vomit, so she knew that she needed a much-needed shower and change of clothes.

"You have to, because she's gonna stay until Van's wedding which is only a few weeks away."

Shaking her head, Scarlet entered the bathroom after grabbing a pair of jeans and t-shirt. She closed the door behind her with a sigh, as she tried to think her way out of even looking at Lauren's face.

"Oh yeah, it's lunch time already, so come down when you're done!" Blake yelled from outside the bathroom which made Scarlet groan again.

The Payne house was buzzing with the fact that Stewart was gone. The men complained of how they had let him go alive, while the women laughed at how he had peed himself. The kids were all bickering with each other about which game they wanted to play while the young adults of the family; Juliet, Blake, Vanessa and

Scarlet, were all sitting in the living room away from the adults, with Lauren and Kevin with them.

"I hate that the kids get to sit with the big people, but we don't." Blake complained as he pouted. "Maybe that's the reason why." Vanessa pointed at him as the others laughed.

"And maybe that's the reason why kids don't like you." Blake retorted as Vanessa glared at him. "You both are such kids." Juliet chimed in as she made faces at Blake. "Hey, hey. No calling my girl a kid." Vanessa smiled at Kevin as he smirked wrapping his free arm around his soon-to-be-bride's shoulders. "Only I can do that."

Everyone laughed as Vanessa slapped Kevin's arm with a pout on her face. Kevin smiled a little before he pecked her lips lovingly making Vanessa smile as well.

Lauren and Scarlet were the only ones that were quietly -- awkwardly -- eating their lunch as everyone around them conversed with laughs and teasing. Scarlet looked at Kevin and Vanessa with a longing look as they only reminded her of how Katie and her were like that too.

"Stop brooding." Blake whispered in Scarlet's ear as he bumped shoulders with her, making her glare at him. "I'm not."

"Yeah, and you aren't sneaking glances at Lauren either." He rolled his eyes at Scarlet, while the girl glared at him. "I feel left out." Juliet whispered from beside Blake while leaning in closer so that she could look at Scarlet as well.

"Eat your food." Scarlet ordered as she turned back to her half-eaten sandwich that looked less appetizing now.

She sighed before getting up from the circle, in which they were sitting in on the carpet, before making her way to the entrance of the living room. Everyone was now looking at her in confusion but she just simply lied, "I feel home sick."

"This is your home, woman." Blake retorted getting a glare from the said girl. "No, New York is." Scarlet mumbled to herself as she went out of the living room and opted to go to the guest room to get a shut eye for a while.

"She's been this way since Stewart showed up." Vanessa sighed and Kevin held her hand, getting an appreciative peck on the cheek from Vanessa. "We know who else to blame." Lauren mumbled to herself as she took a bite of her sandwich before getting up herself.

"Now, where are you going?" Juliet asked as she stared at the blonde woman. "Uh, to pee." Lauren lied with a nervous smile.

"Uh huh, with Scarlet." Blake snorted which made Juliet ram her elbow in Blake's ribs making him groan loudly while clutching the place she brutally assaulted.

Vanessa and Kevin looked at the two weirdly and Lauren took this moment to get out of the living room.

She ascended the stairs with nervousness creeping up inside her while she thought about all the things that Scarlet could do. She could never again talk to Lauren ever again but the most common thought that was finding way into her mind over and over again was the thought that Scarlet could go running back to Katie, and that was what made Lauren afraid.

Reaching the guest room, Lauren found the door open and Scarlet laying on her back on the mattress she was using, with her eyes staring into thin air.

Lauren didn't know what else to do than to knock and that she did, catching Scarlet's attention which was given all to the ceiling.

"Can I come in?" Lauren asked and internally face-palmed herself at the dumb question. Of course, she could. She was using the room too.

Scarlet, instead of answering, turned her back to Lauren. Lauren feeling hurt, stood there awkwardly as she decided in her mind to not enter the room without Scarlet's permission.

Lauren leaned against the door and sighed loudly, trying to catch Scarlet's attention. Unbeknownst to her, Scarlet had all of her attention on the woman without her even trying.

"I won't move away from here, until you say that you want me to enter this room." Lauren spoke as she crossed her arms across her chest.

"Go away." Scarlet groaned out as she placed a stray pillow on her head. "Nope." Lauren shook her head even when she knew that Scarlet couldn't see her do so.

"Everyone I trust just ends up being a liar behind my back." Scarlet muttered and Lauren felt an ache travel through her heart to her head which then commanded her to go to Scarlet, and that she did.

Walking into the room, Lauren plopped beside Scarlet, who in turn scooted away from the blonde woman.

"I'm truly sorry." Lauren apologized but it all went in from one ear and out the other for Scarlet. "Everyone is, when they're caught." Scarlet mumbled sourly as she sighed heavily with the pillow still on her head.

"I never wanted to hurt you, Scar. I just-" Scarlet snorted before she turned to look at Lauren, who was sitting beside her. "And yet you ended up doing it anyway."

"Can you just shut up and listen to me." Lauren snapped and Scarlet glared at her before sitting up to face Lauren better. "You don't get to snap at me. You're the one at fault here."

"I know, but you-" Lauren was cut off again as Scarlet began to speak again. "No, you lied to me. You made me feel like I had a friend that understood me but you were just pretending so that you could get an ice-cream sundae. Was an ice-cream sundae worth more than my feelings to you?" Scarlet looked at Lauren with a look of anger and disbelief. Lauren shook her head and opened her mouth to speak but Scarlet didn't give her a chance.

"And don't even think that I'll forgive you just because we became friends over the past few weeks."

Lauren nodded her head before she placed her palm on Scarlet's mouth making the said girl frown. "Can I speak now, or do you want to talk some more?" Scarlet looked at the green eyes of the woman before she glared at her.

Lauren smiled at her before she scooted a little closer to Scarlet, leaving little to no space between their bodies. Scarlet could've felt Lauren's breath on her lips if she didn't have the blonde's open palm on her mouth.

"I'm sorry." Lauren spoke as she stared deep into Scarlet's eyes and the way that Scarlet's breath hitched was unnoticeable to the blonde woman but Lauren was feeling the exact same way. Her breath was fast and yet she felt a bit breathless as she looked into Scarlet's eyes and Scarlet did the same.

The both of them were so entranced in each other's gazes that they didn't even notice the way they were leaning closer into each other. Lauren's hand slowly moved away from Scarlet's mouth to her cheek.

They were only a breath away from each other and were still leaning closer into each other as if they didn't want any space left between them. Lauren's eyes fell shut as she breathed deeply against Scarlet's lips, making the said girl's eyes to close as well.

Breathing the same air as each other, they were just about to close the little gap when a knock came from the doorway.

Lauren and Scarlet flew away from each other and both of their cheeks were colored a deep red as they looked up to see Blake and Juliet standing beside the open door with similar smirks on their faces.

"Did we disturb something?" Juliet mocked as she smirked at the two women. Lauren groaned before looking at Scarlet, who looked lost in thought. "We could leave and let you continue what you were about to do." Blake jumped into the mocking as his eyebrows wiggled in suggestion.

"No, you didn't disturb anything." Scarlet spoke as she got off the mattress, purposely avoiding Lauren's eyes as she walked to the door where two of her cousins stood.

Looking at the two, Scarlet just sighed and went out of the room, thinking about what she was going to even do and why she was feeling disappointed that it couldn't continue on.

While Lauren, groaned before falling face forward into the pillow. Her heart was beating wildly and her lips were still feeling the warmth that Scarlet's breath had provided her with.

A hand went to touch her lips and a ghost of a smile came onto her face but it quickly disappeared when she thought about how Scarlet would ignore her now, again.

"She looks really disappointed." Juliet commented as she walked over to Lauren with Blake following close behind.

"I hate you both." Lauren spoke loud enough for the two to hear and they both glanced at each other before they smiled widely.

In the moment, both Lauren and Scarlet had one thing on their mind. Each other's lips.

Chapter 9

It was night time, and as usual, the Payne household was buzzing with conversation, games and mostly the wedding planning since it was only two weeks away now.

Kevin and Vanessa were both going to have their Bachelor's party a day before their wedding and even though Kevin was against the idea of even having a bachelor's party in the first place, Blake had convinced him otherwise.

Scarlet and Lauren were still not talking but since the wedding was so close, they were piled up with preparations and didn't even feel the need to converse.

Everyone was busy in doing something that concerned the wedding ceremony.

Blake and Scarlet had gone to buy their suits because they were the only ones that still had nothing to wear. Lauren and Juliet had gone to buy dresses with the Payne women when Blake and Scarlet weren't home, so they couldn't go with them.

"How does this one look?" Blake held out another black suit as he looked at his cousin who looked bored. Since, the wedding had no such thing as a dress code, Scarlet and Blake were told to select any suit that they liked.

Scarlet was done with selecting her suit, she was just waiting for Blake to decide, which he was finding hard to do.

"That's the sixth black suit. It's good though, just like the previous five." Scarlet mumbled as she looked at Blake with a bored look.

"You could at least humor me." Blake pouted as he went back to the racks of suits lined up. Scarlet sighed before she got her phone out of her jeans pocket.

Going to the contact list, Scarlet scrolled down to the name she had on her mind ever since the almost kiss that Lauren and her shared. She was deciding if she should call or not, it's not like she would know who called her.

Scarlet had changed her phone when she came to her hometown, with only her heart just the same. Everything else was different, her hairstyle, her clothing style, her attitude to things in life, everything was different than the time she left her hometown to pursue a career in the magazine industry.

She had promised herself to never regret her decisions but here she was, regretting them more than anything. She regretted ever meeting Stewart, ever working for him, ever bumping into Katie at the diner she frequented. But most of all, she regretted ever meeting Lauren, who she met at a photo shoot.

Lauren had looked beautiful at the time with her face clean of makeup and her smile just as bright as ever. Scarlet would've asked for the model's number if she hadn't already gotten a girlfriend.

But now, when Katie had broken her trust and her heart, Scarlet couldn't help but to think if she could have something with Lauren.

They were just about to kiss when her two annoying cousins interrupted them.

Shaking her head from all those thoughts, she tapped the name and stood up while placing the phone to her ear.

Scarlet glanced at Blake who was busy looking at suits, before she stepped out of the store. The ringing was still there, and Scarlet was now beginning to wonder if she would pick up her phone or not.

Blake, noticed that Scarlet wasn't in the store anymore, and decided to investigate as to where she went. He found her standing outside the store and the way Scarlet was close to the door, he could hear everything.

"Hey......Katie?" The way Blake's eyes widened, it felt like they were going to pop right out. Scarlet had a serious look on her face as she began to walk away from the store.

Blake looked at her leave through the doorway of the store, but didn't follow her. He had heard enough.

"Are you buying this one?" A male worker came over to him and asked with a polite smile sent his way. Blake nodded and the worker began to walk over to the paying area.

Taking a glance over his shoulder, he followed the worker. "And the other one as well." He spoke up to the worker, who nodded in acknowledgement.

"Oh, honey, Blake and Scar are back!" Laura yelled, and Andrew yelled an 'okay' back to his wife, when she opened the front door.

The house was impossibly silent and this caught Scarlet's attention as she began to look around the house after entering. "Is everyone dead?" She joked and got a slap on the arm by her mother.

Blake chuckled as he just went to go upstairs. He had to tell Juliet and Lauren that Scarlet had called Katie.

Reaching the top of the stairs, he rushed to the guest room. The door was already open, and both the girls were sitting there with a board game out, focused on it.

Blake went over to them, and flipped the board with all of his strength getting a smile from Lauren and a curse word from Juliet, when their board turned over.

"What the actual fuck, Blake?" Juliet glared at him as she glanced at the sabotaged game now. "And I was winning."

"Oh, trust me, I have something more interesting than a stupid board game." Blake spoke as he sat down on the mattress where the two were sat, on his knees.

"What is it?" Lauren asked as her curiosity sky rocketed.

"Don't humor him, he always has something interesting to tell when in reality it's the complete opposite." Juliet rolled her eyes, making Blake cross his arms over his chest in defense.

"Oh well, then I won't tell you how Scar called a certain ex of hers when we were out buying suits." Lauren and Juliet, both, looked at him shocked as he looked away from them with a smirk on his face.

"You already did." Juliet spoke as she glanced at Lauren, who had a frown on her face. "What did you hear, exactly?"

"I just know that Scar called Katie, but before I could listen on to her conversation, she just walked away." Blake explained making Lauren frown some more, if that was even possible.

"Maybe, she called to dump her." Juliet shrugged. "Or to invite her to the wedding and get back together." Blake spoke which got him a glare from Juliet when Lauren looked at him with complete horror on her face.

"What? It's a possibility and besides what else could she do than to take her back. You lied to her." Juliet face-palmed when Blake kept talking before she flicked him on the forehead, but it was too late since the damage was already done.

Lauren felt worse than she did the day before. She blamed herself for everything now, she was at fault. She shouldn't have lied to Scarlet, and she regretted it now.

"As long as she's happy, it's okay." Lauren spoke with a cracked voice before she began to silently sob. Juliet comforted her new friend by caressing her back.

"Hey, you can't just give up. And besides, Scar is an idiot. I'll just go hit her upside on her head and she'll come back to her senses and beg you to be with her." Lauren shook her head while Blake began to comfort her as well by awkwardly patting her back.

While, this all was happening, Scarlet was stood outside the door with her back pressed against the wall, as she was deep in thought.

She hadn't heard all of their conversation but she had heard the important parts and was ready to stop running.

Lauren was sitting on the rooftop, where she had found Scarlet sitting only a few days earlier, when she was hiding from her. The whole irony of the situation was, that now their roles were reversed. Lauren was hiding from Scarlet.

Her head was rested on her knees as her legs were pulled up to her chest.

It was dark out, and downstairs, the Payne men were preparing dinner since it was their turn to. Ever since, the whole family had united, they were taking turns in making dinner. And tonight, was the men's turn.

Downstairs, Scarlet was searching through the house for the blonde woman that she wanted to talk to but couldn't find anywhere.

Juliet and Blake were sitting in the living room talking over old-movies while the women were all gathered around the coffee table playing monopoly, including Vanessa. The kids were upstairs in the guest bedroom playing with their action figures and Granny Payne, was in her room sleeping just like most of the time.

"Have you guys seen Lauren?" Juliet and Blake, both looked at Scarlet with one of their eyebrows up with question. Sometimes, Scarlet thought that Blake and Juliet were actually twins that were born three years apart and to different mothers.

"Why?" Blake was the one that asked, and got a frown from Scarlet. "Do you know where she is or not?" Juliet smirked at her before she shook her head. "Nope."

Scarlet glared at the two before she left to go search for her upstairs. "She's on the rooftop." Kevin whispered as he walked by Scarlet. She looked at him give her a wink as he went back to the kitchen.

'Great, does everyone around here know that I'm a lesbian, am I that damn obvious?' Scarlet thought as she frowned before a mischievous smile came on to her face.

"Aunt Wanda, Blake is a man too. He should be cooking as well." Scarlet turned around and walked up the stairs as she heard Wanda order Blake to go help the other male members of the family. Blake whined and yelled at Scarlet just as she laughed loudly.

Going up to the rooftop, Scarlet breathed deeply before she felt the wind blow against her face just as she waked through the small doorway of the rooftop, brushing her medium length hair from over her eyes, Scarlet walked out to the rooftop. She came over and sat down beside Lauren, who had her face turned the other way and hadn't noticed the presence of the older woman.

"It's cold." Scarlet stated, catching Lauren's attention as she turned her head to look at a smiling Scarlet. "You look cold."

Lauren shook her head before she turned her head to look at the sky now. "Why are you here?" Lauren asked as she sighed out. "Because I had no choice, my mother had to push me out. I couldn't have just lived inside her."

Lauren looked at Scarlet with a serious face while Scarlet smiled awkwardly while rubbing her neck. "Too soon?"

"Too soon."

Scarlet sighed before she scooted closer to the blonde woman and draped an arm over her shoulder, to keep her warm. Lauren, confused by the action looked at her and noticed just how much close they were now.

Scarlet and Lauren were only an inch away from each other's lips. And the way Scarlet was breathing through her slightly parted lips, Lauren could feel the warm air hitting her own and her eyes involuntarily closed just as her lips parted.

"I'm sorry for leading you on." Lauren's eyes opened immediately and she looked into the older woman's eyes in confusion. "You didn't." Lauren spoke as she started to scoot a bit further away from Scarlet, but Scarlet didn't loosen her hold on her, instead pulled her even closer.

"You're not a rebound, and I don't want to promise you my heart and soul, when I can only give you my attention." Lauren listened attentively as Scarlet brought a hand up to stroke her cheek lovingly.

"You deserve better than me, I can't even give you the broken pieces of my heart. Everything still belongs to Katie." Scarlet's eyes began to fill up with tears as she looked into the green ones of Lauren.

Her eyes weren't blue like Katie's and her hair wasn't dyed blonde. Her eyes didn't show her the vast oceans and the sky in its purest form, but her eyes did show her the deepest of forests that were wrapping countless of vines and branches around her, promising to never let her go.

"But I can try." Those words were all that Scarlet needed to admit before she brought Lauren's face even closer to hers. She breathed against her lips, glancing from her eyes to her lips, asking for permission as her heart thudded aggressively against her chest.

Lauren tried hard to not show the smile that was trying to show on her face as she controlled her wildly racing heart, before she finally touched Scarlet's lips with her own.

It was a kiss that was all over the place, as Lauren's hand came up to hold on to Scarlet's neck so that even if the older woman tried, she couldn't back away from her lips.

Scarlet smiled between the kiss before her arm wrapped itself around the blonde's waist. Lips moving and tongues meeting in a battle that was dominated by Lauren for a while before Scarlet began to control it.

Lauren smiled even after trying to control it from coming on to her lips and their lips broke off.

Scarlet's eyes opened and this was the first time that she didn't see the blue after an intense kiss, and saw green instead. But the warm and loving green was enough for her to lean in again and claim her lips in another battle, this one a little slower and deeper than the first one.

"I'm still mad at you for lying." Scarlet smiled as she spoke breathlessly as she broke off the kiss. Lauren looked at Scarlet while trying to catch her breath.

Suddenly, she remembered what Blake had told her and she scooted away from Scarlet as fast as she could, leaving Scarlet with confusion. "Why did you call Katie today?"

Scarlet expected the question so she wasn't as much shocked as Lauren was when she told her the reason why, "I wanted to officially tell her that we were done."

Lauren's eyes softened and she bowed her head a little before she moved back closer to Scarlet without anything said, as she blushed embarrassingly. "Are you blushing?"

Lauren kept her head down and Scarlet laughed a little before she hugged Lauren, pulling the blonde close to her chest. "You are so cute."

Lauren groaned but deep inside she was happy, scratch that, she was more than happy. And the only thing that was causing her this much happiness was the fact that Scarlet was going to try – just for her.

Like she was special. Truly, she believed in that moment, that she was indeed special.

Chapter 10

When the two had come down from their high – literally – only the two annoying cousins looked at them suspiciously, as if they had just made out for a whole half-an-hour.

Unknown to the two cousins, that was certainly the case here.

The whole time during dinner, Lauren and Scarlet kept glancing at each other like love struck teenagers, and the only thing that was wrong with the whole situation was the fact that they glanced at each other when the other wasn't looking, making it seem like a scene straight out of a movie, about an unrequited love.

After dinner, the male members of the family were praised for their great cooking skills by the women and the children.

The desert was bought from the superstore that was near their house, which was a huge tub of chocolate ice-cream, which was Granny Payne's favorite.

Pudding was yipping in her lap while she savored every bite of her small scoop of ice-cream since she was only allowed a little.

When everything was done with, and Blake and Kevin were ordered to wash the dishes, everyone moved into the living room.

Lauren and Scarlet, however, took the excuse of being tired and went up to the guest room with shy smiles sent each other's way.

"Can we cuddle again now?" Scarlet asked just as she plopped down on to her mattress where she slept alone. "You are such a great human pillow."

"And you are always so warm." Lauren spoke as she sat down next to Scarlet, who went to lay down on her back with her hands tucked underneath her head. She stared up at Lauren with an adoring stare before she patted the space beside her as if telling Lauren to lay down as well.

Lauren smiled adorably before laying down beside the older woman. She snuggled closer to Scarlet's body, as she placed her head, on top of Scarlet's arm with her own arm wrapped around her torso.

"Do you remember the time when we first met?" Lauren asked all of a sudden as she closed her eyes and entangled her own legs with Scarlet's. "When you were wearing that awful dress in the name of fashion."

Lauren raised her head up and looked at Scarlet in disbelief. "That was my first photo shoot, first-timers get awful dresses." Scarlet smiled before she pecked Lauren's forehead, getting a blush from the blonde.

"I wanted to get your digits but I had a girlfriend so......" Scarlet trailed off with a frown, and Lauren, judging by the instant silence, raised her head again and looked at Scarlet.

"Let's introduce ourselves again." Lauren excitedly spoke as she sat up completely getting a confused look from the older woman, as she sat up as well.

"Hi, I'm Lauren. I'm 21 years old and I work as a model. My favorite color is pink." Lauren brought her hand in front of Scarlet, for her to shake.

Scarlet chuckled before she shook the blonde's hand while speaking, "Hey Lauren, I'm Scarlet. I'm older than you and at the moment, I'm unemployed. And my favorite color is blue." Lauren smiled brightly as Scarlet stopped talking. "See, now, you can ask for my number."

"But, I already have your number." Lauren frowned before she grabbed Scarlet's phone from under the pillow. "Hey, how'd you know I keep it there?" Scarlet questioned in disbelief as Lauren smirked before she shrugged. "Secret."

Scarlet simply shook her head with a smile on her face as she watched the blonde tap away on her phone. After a while of tapping here and there, Lauren handed the phone to Scarlet.

"What did you do?" Scarlet asked as she began to look at her phone with a raised eyebrow. "Oh, I just deleted my number and then re-added it."

Laughing, Scarlet just brought her arms around the blonde's shoulders and embraced her completely. They fell on their sides, still embracing each other as Lauren began to giggle adorably.

They didn't know when, but they fell asleep in each other's arms, with their legs tangled together and their faces holding content smiles.

When Blake and Juliet came to sleep, they saw the two women cuddling and cooed at the sight before they took several photos. Greg was sad that he wasn't invited to the cuddle party but he still went ahead and cuddled with Scarlet's back, since she was laying on her side.

The twins were indifferent to the whole situation, that they just went to sleep.

Waking up, Scarlet noticed a lot of things. Like first-of-all, how Lauren had her whole body atop of Scarlet's and was snoring lightly. The other thing that she noticed was the way Greg was on the other half of her body that Lauren hadn't occupied yet.

She was underneath the body weight of two people but still, she was enjoying herself. She knew how Greg got jealous when someone else was taking his place, and this time Lauren was the one that was taking his place.

Scarlet yawned with the after-effects of sleeping before she looked at the two pair of eyes that were staring at her.

"Had a good night's sleep?" Juliet smirked as she asked with sarcasm dripping from her mouth. Scarlet rolled her eyes at her cousins before she tried to feel her arms that were wrapped around both Lauren and Greg's bodies.

"You know, we took some great pictures. We could use them for blackmail."

Scarlet squinted her eyes at the two before she spoke, "You wouldn't."

Blake nodded with a smirk, "We totally would." Scarlet glared at the two for a while, and both the cousins felt uncomfortable under the glare of Scarlet, before they broke. "Okay, okay. We won't."

Scarlet smirked and heard a little giggle from the blonde woman that was now trying to sit up on the mattress but was failing because of the arm that kept pulling her back.

"I need to pee." Lauren whined and, Juliet and Blake laughed with snorts. Scarlet stared at the blonde woman before she smirked and let the blonde go.

"You two are so cute together." Juliet cooed which made Lauren blush deeply, but before anyone could notice, she rushed into the bathroom after getting off of the mattress.

"You two are so annoying." Scarlet spoke as she threw a stray pillow at the two cousins getting a laugh from Blake and a scream from Juliet.

Greg, who was in scarlet's arms, stirred before he woke up with a loud whine. "Look what you did, you woke him up." Juliet pointed at a now awake Greg. "Me? You were the one that screamed like a witch." Scarlet smirked when she saw her younger cousin open her mouth, ready to fight with Scarlet.

Greg, on the other hand, glared at Juliet before he went out of the room, maybe to find his mother – Wanda.

In the bathroom, Lauren was washing her hands after doing her business and was also laughing at the two cousins' bickering which she could hear clearly.

Juliet and Scarlet were still having a verbal combat when Vanessa rushed into the room and slammed the door shut before locking it.

"What the…?" Scarlet was cut off by a deathly look that Vanessa threw her way. "Don't even finish that sentence." She warned with a finger before she sighed.

Juliet and Blake glanced at each other before they looked at Vanessa with curious stares. "Why are you in the peasants' room?" Blake teased as he arched an eyebrow in question while looking at the oldest cousin in the family.

"Kevin's parents are here, earlier than expected." She spoke with a worried expression as she brought her fingers to her mouth before biting on her nails. A nervous habit that she had developed in her teenage years.

"So? What does that have to do with us?" Juliet asked as she crossed her arms across her chest. "Well, they are extremely judgmental and annoying. And also, they prey on young people."

"Okay, that's a bit of exaggeration." Scarlet laughed as she got off of the mattress and walked over to her sister. "Kevin's a nice guy and I'm guessing his parents are nice people too."

Vanessa smiled nervously at her sister.

"Okay, I take it back. They prey on young people." Scarlet whispered harshly into Vanessa's ear as she tried to pry off the dog that kept climbing up her leg.

There was one thing that Scarlet couldn't handle, and that was attention. And at the moment, the whole living room had its attention on her, as in, everyone was conversing about her – even Granny Payne.

Lauren was enjoying everything as she was sat beside Granny Payne that was talking about all of the embarrassing days that Scarlet had encountered in her life, as if they were scenes from a comedy film.

Scarlet looked at Granny Payne in horror before she mouthed, 'traitor' to Lauren, that was laughing pretty loudly at the embarrassing moments of Scarlet.

Before Scarlet had found herself being the center of attention, she was introduced to Mrs. Anderson - Kevin's mother. On first glance, Scarlet had come to a conclusion that Vanessa was indeed exaggerating when she defined Kevin's parents. In fact, they were incredibly sweet and easy-going.

That all changed when Mr. Anderson asked Scarlet a simple life related question, "Are you in a relationship, child?" That was the initiation of the whole, 'let's talk about Scarlet' movement.

Before Scarlet could answer, Laura jumped into the conversation, "She was cheated on by her boyfriend, so she's single now." Mr. and Mrs. Anderson shook their heads in pity while looking at Scarlet, who in that moment was awkwardly smiling at the couple.

"Nice boys these days are hard to find." Mr. Anderson commented as he clicked his tongue in distaste after his sentence. "They play hard to get."

"Yes, and there must be something that you had done to have such a thing happen to you, darling." Scarlet wanted to scowl at the woman that was implying that being cheated on was Scarlet's own fault. Lauren looked at Scarlet with worry as she shifted in her seat beside Granny Payne.

"Wait a minute. It wasn't Scarlet's fault that the boy cheated on her." Andrew, Scarlet's father, came to her defense as he piped in the conversation with a frown. "The boy seemed like trouble just from the first look."

Laura nodded her head in agreement as she looked at Mrs. Anderson. "Well, whatever the outcome now, don't worry. We'll help you find a great hunky man." Mrs. Anderson went from pitiful to excited in a minute. Scarlet, cringed subtly as she wondered if people used the word 'hunky' nowadays.

"She can't keep a man by her side for long. Not with her manly charm, anyways."

"Mother!" Uncle Jared yelled at her for saying such a thing but she just shrugged innocently. "It's not like there's no truth in it."

Andrew placed a hand on Uncle Jared's shoulder as he was about to say something else at his mother's words.

Scarlet sighed when Vanessa grabbed a hold of her hand and squeezed as to show her support.

Mr. and Mrs. Anderson glanced at each other before they looked at Scarlet. "You do need a makeover." Mrs. Anderson muttered and that's how Granny Payne and her friendship bloomed.

And now, Scarlet was cringing at the old high school stories of herself that Granny Payne and Laura were sharing with Mrs. Anderson while laughing heartily. Lauren was amongst them as well as she was giggling now and then when she would hear something terribly humiliating that happened to Scarlet once upon a time.

"Your love life is going downhill, man." Blake whispered in Scarlet's ear as he was now occupying the place where Vanessa was sat a while ago. Now, Vanessa was out with Kevin discussing about something serious.

Scarlet gave him a side glare before she sighed, "I will never be able to live this down." She ran her hand down her face. "Dude, are you crying?" Blake asked as he poked Scarlet in the ribs. "No, I'm laughing. At myself, if you're wondering. I just.... I had such bad luck back then." Scarlet spoke as she wiped a stray tear away.

Not far from them, Granny Payne was trying hard to laugh and speak at the same time, "And that one time when she peed herself in school." Scarlet made a horrified expression at that as she quickly got up from the couch and went over to the four women that were having a great time discussing about all of her embarrassing moments.

"Lauren, I need your help." She spoke as she smiled politely at the three women charmingly. "Why?" Lauren whined as she looked over at Granny Payne. "She was just getting to the good part."

Scarlet shook her head before she grabbed Lauren by the arm and dragged her away from the three women that just laughed at the red-faced Scarlet, as she escaped from the living room with the blonde woman in tow.

"Where are we going?" Lauren asked as Scarlet took her up the stairs and then into the guest room. Closing the door after entering the room, Scarlet leaned against it before taking a breath of relief.

"I didn't know you did ballet." Lauren giggled as she spoke. Scarlet groaned before face-palming, "Only for a month."

"It still counts for something." Lauren smiled at the woman that was blushing madly as she tried to look away from the blonde.

"Yeah, if you consider the brutal remarks of my instructor or the way I almost broke all of my toes." The exaggeration in Scarlet's voice was noticeable to both of them as they both burst out laughing just a minute later.

"I hated that pink tutu." Scarlet added as she grabbed Lauren's hand and tugged her towards herself. "I would love to see you in a tutu." Scarlet frowned when Lauren laughed at her. "Don't say that in front of my mom, she'd take those old albums out and you'll have pictures for all those embarrassing times as well."

The way Lauren's eyes sparkled made Scarlet regret about even telling the blonde that there was photographic proof of it as well.

Scarlet groaned loudly and Lauren laughed before she placed her arms around Scarlet's shoulders. "I used to do ballet too." This caught Scarlet's attention and she raised a questioning eyebrow at the blonde woman. "Judging by the gracefulness of your body, I'm guessing you didn't stop after a month."

Lauren blushed before she spoke, "You observe my body."

"Yeah, well. Before, I had a job to do. But now, I just look at your body when you aren't noticing." Lauren opened her mouth in surprise before she closed it and squinted her eyes at the older woman.

"Are your hormones on a regular level?" Scarlet burst out laughing while Lauren glared at her. "What? Answer me."

"You......you think I'm horny." It was a statement, rather than a question which made Lauren's cheek color themselves a deep red. "Y-Yeah well, a normal person wouldn't look at other peoples' bodies if they weren't horny."

Scarlet shook her head as a soft smile came on to her face, "I meant that I look at the way your body moves when you do as little as pour milk into a glass."

The blonde's blush didn't disappear when Scarlet wrapped her arms around her waist and pulled her closer to her own body. "I like how graceful you are in everything that you do. And to answer your previous question, yes. I am really horny."

Lauren stared at Scarlet with her mouth agape as she tried to move out of Scarlet's hold subtly. Scarlet, who was joking, pulled the blonde closer and brought their lips close.

"I really want you." Scarlet whispered against Lauren's lips making the blonde's breath hitch. "I-I...." Lauren was lost for words as her mouth opened and then closed as if she was a fish out of water.

Scarlet, seeing the effects that she was causing in Lauren, laughed after pulling away from the blonde leaving Lauren at a loss of warmth.

"I was just kidding." Scarlet spoke as she looked at Lauren, who was now looking at the ground with mixed emotions. She wasn't ready to sleep with Scarlet, but at the same time, she was more than ready to claim her as hers. And between all of this, she was confused as to what to do.

"Hey, are you okay?" Scarlet asked as she placed a hand on Lauren's arm to bring her out of her thoughts. Lauren glanced at Scarlet before she blushed and nodded her head. "Yeah, I'm fine."

"Okay then." Scarlet spoke awkwardly as she opened the door and walked out of it before offering a hand towards Lauren.

Lauren glanced form the hand to Scarlet, and decided in her head.

Taking Scarlet's offered hand, she smiled and got out of the room as well.

'I'll be ready when she'll be.'

Chapter 11

It was chaos, the whole Payne household was in chaos when the second last week before the wedding day arrived. Kevin's parents were now staying in a nearby hotel and were doing their best to prepare for the wedding without visiting the Payne household regularly.

Scarlet and Vanessa, both, were ecstatic when Kevin told this news. Scarlet had the urge to kiss him but refrained from doing so.

Blake was being the best brother-in-law for Kevin since he was the one that was organizing his bachelor party for him, with strippers and food and strippers and food, because that was the only two things he had in mind.

Juliet on the other hand, was given the responsibility to throw the best bachelorette party that anyone had ever seen. Taking it seriously, Juliet had kept it a surprise from the ladies what she had organized and was excited for it.

Scarlet and Lauren, had grown closer in the days following up to the two bachelor parties, and were keeping things simple and slow, with light caresses here and there but heavy kissing behind doors.

For Scarlet, things were going great. She hadn't thought about Katie in a long while and was finding herself falling face first in a hole that she was greatly familiar with, called love. The only thing she was afraid of now was the thought of giving all of her to Lauren. That was what kept her awake with thoughts sometimes at night.

She was afraid and this time there was nowhere to run to. It was do or die, and in this case, stay or leave.

"I'll miss you after the wedding." Blake spoke to Scarlet with a pout on his face, as they both were sitting at a park bench. It was in the middle of the day and the two cousins had found themselves going out for a midday stroll.

Unknown to Scarlet, this stroll was for a deep conversation on Blake's part. He wanted to discuss a rather touchy subject with her and was afraid she might blow up on him if it was discussed in the house, surrounded by the whole family and not to forget, Lauren.

"Oh come on, we'll keep in touch." Scarlet bumped her shoulders with Blake and he managed to place a smile on his face before he raised his head up to look at the sky which was clean of clouds.

Surely, it was a great day to be out.

"But, it won't be like these moments." Scarlet raised an eyebrow at her cousin who was suddenly behaving out of character. A guy, who was always so easy going and careless was here beside her worrying about what the future held. A guy like him, who was even doubtful of the existence of tomorrow was wondering how it would be.

"Are you okay?" Scarlet teased as she placed her open palm on his forehead to check for a fever. "I'm okay." He retorted as he poked his elbow into Scarlet's ribs getting a mix of a laugh and wince from the woman.

"I was just thinking."

"A penny for your thoughts?" Scarlet spoke as she stared off into the park's distance. Memories came to her when she looked around the park. Memories that she neither wanted to treasure nor forget. Speaking of memories, the whole town brought back those things that people remember when they come back to a certain place.

"When will you tell them?" Blake asked with his best serious voice and face as he turned to stare at his cousin, who was now staring at thin air, thinking of how to not question that question. "Tell who what?"

Blake rolled his eyes before he sighed, "The rest of the family about being a lesbian." Scarlet knew that one day or another she would've been asked that question but she was expecting that question from Katie, not from her own cousin.

"Why?" Scarlet answered in a question and this time Blake turned his whole body towards Scarlet. "They deserve to know." Scarlet rolled her eyes at him before she turned to look at him as well. "They deserve to know what I see fit for them to know." Blake didn't understand what that was supposed to mean but he tried to play it off by giving her a glare.

"They are your family, at least tell your parents if not everyone."

"Look, Blake. I came out here to find peace, not to have a verbal fight with you on the topic of telling my parents about how their daughter isn't a dick lover." Blake wanted to gasp at her but refrained from doing so and instead grabbed her shoulders and shook her with all his might.

"They need to know, you idiot."

"Who in the name of hell are you calling an idiot?" Scarlet growled as she slapped both of his hands away from her. "I don't have to answer to anyone and besides, after the wedding, I'm going to go back to New York. I only came here to get away from Katie."

"I didn't know you were so selfish." Blake crossed his arms, and Scarlet gave him a hard glare. "I'm not selfish, okay. I just don't want them to know."

"Because you're afraid." It wasn't a question, more like a statement which Scarlet didn't like at all. "I'm not afraid. I just...."

Blake looked at her, with a soft look in his eyes and sighed before he patted her back while leaning back on the bench. "You have to tell them someday or another."

It was true. She had to tell them someday. But the thought of having to deal with the outcome of her actions was what held her back. She was afraid of being shunned by her family even though she was quite sure that most of them wouldn't even care if she liked girls or not.

But when a certain grey haired woman came into mind, she shivered with the results that would pile up in her head. The old woman already loathed her presence, Scarlet didn't want her to not even want to face her anymore.

She knew that her grandmother wasn't the best of grandmothers out there, but she was her grandmother and she, despite knowing her hatred, loved her.

"It's the perfect time to come out, everyone's here. And I know that everyone wouldn't care if you like dicks or vaginas, they would still love you." Blake spoke and Scarlet gave him a watery smile before shaking her head.

"You expect me to believe that Vanessa would still love me after knowing that I'm gay, when she was the girl that screamed bloody murder when she found out that I had a measly crush on a girl. If I remember correctly, she was the one that had teared up my limited-edition poster of Selena Gomez." Blake laughed but then realized what Scarlet was telling him, and immediately sobered up with a serious face on his face.

"Oh come one, that must've been long ago when she was a naïve child."

"That was when she was 20 and I was 18." Scarlet gave Blake an unamused stare. "She's not the same woman anymore."

Scarlet narrowed her eyes at him before she shook her head, "And not to forget that our grandmother hates me."

"That's just....... not true." Scarlet raised an eyebrow at him and he bowed his head down. "Well, except for those two, we all love you and would accept you."

"Your father, Blake. Uncle Jared."

Both Blake and Scarlet's chins tipped a little upwards as they imagined how Uncle Jared was when he had found out that same-sex marriage was legal in all the states of America.

"America has turned queer. Everyone's a damn homosexual. I swear if I just see one of them in front of my own eyes, I'd.... I'd have a long and hard talk with them."

Shivers ran up their bodies just even thinking about that long and hard talk. Who knew what he would talk about even? Maybe he'd just show gay people straight porn if things went his way, while continuously saying, "Now this is how it's done."

Another shiver ran up their bodies and they looked at each other. Blake sighed a defeated sigh before he gave Scarlet a frown. "Then what do we do."

"We don't need to do anything." Scarlet replied as she leaned back on the bench as well. "I'm not coming out."

Blake rolled his eyes before he gave her a glare, "What if they found out on their own? What then?"

"That is for when it would happen. Right now, there is nothing to think about." Scarlet spoke before she crossed her arms and stared at the little child that was now swinging on the swing set with his father pushing from behind him.

"But honestly speaking, I'd really miss you after the wedding." Blake spoke as he looked over at the father and son as well. Scarlet smiled before she threw an arm around Blake's shoulder and brought him in a loving hug.

"I'd miss you too, bug."

Chapter 12

Silence never did suit the Payne household and a specific type of silence when the whole house was fast asleep, well that is, except for a certain dark haired woman.

Scarlet was awake and restless as she turned over on her mattress multiple times, just not finding comfort in any position. A sigh escaped her lips as she looked over at where Lauren was asleep, which was just beside Scarlet's mattress.

Lauren looked peaceful and comfortable, unlike the dark-haired woman who even tried to lay down without a pillow under her head.

At times like these, when she had no distraction, her mind wandered to the nights when she held Katie in her arms and would stroke her hair just to fall asleep.

Memories of the woman with dyed blonde hair, lying in her arms and looking up at her, invaded her head and she just wanted to smash her head against something to make it stop.

When Scarlet did think about it, everything was so easy with Katie. They both liked each other, they both started dating just after meeting once, they even had sex on the third date. But the way Scarlet had fallen in love with Katie wasn't easy. She had denied her feelings, and even tried to suppress them by working more than she should.

But in the end, her feelings were triumphant and she fell deeply in love with the woman.

Now, when Scarlet laid sleepless and restless, trying to just let the darkness consume her and put her to sleep, she went back to the day when she had found Katie and Stewart laying on the same bed – Katie and her shared – after sex.

This time her heart clenched and a certain sadness fell over her, replaced by the anger that was directed towards the two. She wondered what she had done wrong to have received such a cruel punishment.

Thinking back to the times she spent with her, she tried to find just a single flaw in her behavior, a single mistake on her part that had led to such consequences.

And when the rage died down, the insecurity surfaced and Scarlet found herself blaming herself for her broken relationship.

"Hey." Scarlet jolted out of her thoughts as she looked beside her to see the blonde looking at her with worry filled eyes. "Are you okay?" She asked in a whisper and Scarlet gave her a small smile before nodding.

Lauren, frowning, shook her head before she repositioned herself in her make shift bed. "You're lying." She accused in a hushed tone and was rewarded with a small laugh from the dark-haired woman.

"Did I wake you up?" Scarlet laid on her side with her arm underneath her head, so she could gaze at the blonde without any difficulty.

The darkness was spread around the room, but they could still see each other's eyes and the outline of their bodies.

"No, I just felt like someone was watching me." Lauren spoke before she, too, got on her side. "I never pegged you as a creep." Scarlet smiled before she shook her head with humor.

"I wasn't looking at you." She lied and Lauren nodded her head not believing a single word that she muttered. "What were you thinking about there, looking at the ceiling?"

Scarlet frowned before she sighed, "You don't want to know." Her voice came out quieter than before as she stared into the blonde's eyes.

"Were you thinking about Katie?" Lauren frowned back as she asked the dark-haired woman, who went silent before speaking a low 'yes'.

The next thing that Scarlet knew was that she was being pushed on her mattress a little and then a weight dropped beside her. Lauren grabbed Scarlet's arm before placing it underneath her own head and then snuggling comfortably into Scarlet's side.

Scarlet wanted to laugh and she would've if the next thing she heard wasn't so heart-breaking, "Don't go back to Katie." Lauren's voice was a bit cracked and silent but Scarlet immediately leveled herself with Lauren's face and wiped away at her cheek.

"I won't." Scarlet whispered back to her as she placed her arm around the blonde's waist and pulled her into her own body.

"I can't help but wonder, that you'll go back to Katie once you realize that you can't love me back." Lauren's broken voice reached

Scarlet's ears and she wanted to ask what she meant about 'love me back', but instead spoke something entirely different, "I've never kissed Katie on a rooftop before, neither have I ever introduced her to my family." Scarlet paused as she saw Lauren's eyes that held confusion.

"I did that all with you, because you're special and you were there for me when I had no one. Even if you were just trying to get me to go back to New York for an ice-cream sundae." Scarlet's voice held humor and Lauren sniffed.

"I didn't even take a sip of alcohol when Katie cheated on me and yet when you lied to me, I took a swing of a whole bottle." This time Lauren giggled and Scarlet smiled.

"You even puked in Stewart's car." Lauren added as she giggled a bit more. Scarlet nodded with the same smile on her face. "I'm sorry for calling you Katie back then."

Lauren shook her head before snuggling in Scarlet's neck and breathing in her scent. "It's okay. I'm sorry for lying to you."

"That's okay. Your lie brought you here and that's what counts." Scarlet spoke as she pecked the blonde's forehead before sighing in content. A yawn escaped her mouth and she brought Lauren's body closer to her.

"Are you sleepy now?" Lauren asked as she placed a lingering kiss on the exposed skin in front of her and Scarlet nodded. "Yeah, but if you keep doing that, I might just do something else."

Lauren's breath hitched and her mind immediately wandered to what this 'something else' would be.

Looking up at the dark-haired woman, Lauren noticed the close proximity of the two and was about to comment on it when Scarlet brought her lips close to Lauren's.

Whispering as low as she could, Scarlet spoke, "I'm sleepy."

That was not what Lauren had expected to come out of Scarlet's mouth and when a second later, Scarlet had her in her arms, snoring lightly, she just sighed out with a smile.

"You make my heart race." It was a sweet declaration that was confessed in such a way that wasn't burdening or uncomfortable. Truly, love sometimes was a burden but in this case, it was the exact opposite, since it was pushing the baggage off of Scarlet's shoulders that didn't seem to budge.

It seemed as though both of them were the cure to each other's insecurities that found themselves surfacing in the spread of darkness.

In the darkness, there was possibility of finding light. Just like in the depth of a deep green forest, there is possibility of finding life. You just have to look around.

The next morning, Juliet and Blake woke up to find two certain women all cuddled up into each other. They just glanced at each other before they broke out into grins.

The kids were all up as well and had noticed their cousin cuddling with Lauren, but chose to ignore it.

The two cousins, Juliet and Blake, tip-toed into the bathroom with mischievous smiles on their faces. When they came out, they were sporting a bucket full of water which was carried by both of them.

With a single snicker, they dumped all of the contents in the bucket over the two cuddling women, who woke up with gasps and screams as they were drenched with water.

Juliet and Blake burst into laughter but it was quite short-lived because in the next moment, Scarlet was tackling Blake.

Lauren, who was still looking at her now wet clothes in confusion, turned to look at the two cousins that were now having a pillow fight.

"I will kill you!" Scarlet exclaimed as she kept hitting Blake with a pillow, while he laughed holding onto his sides. "Uncle, uncle! I give!" He spoke in between laughter with breathlessness as he tried to push away his cousin from over his body.

"Oh come on, let the kid go. It was just a prank." Juliet spoke as she tried to pry Scarlet off of Blake, still laughing at her cousins.

Scarlet got off of Blake with a last assault before throwing a glare at both of her cousins. Lauren was now off of the wet mattress and was shivering slightly as she looked at the three cousins with a small smile on her face.

"You two better sleep with one eye open tonight." Scarlet spoke in her most menacing tone as she gave them both a mean smile, which made both of them shudder with fear before they rushed out of the room.

"You didn't have to scare them so much." Lauren giggled before she shivered noticeably. Scarlet gave her a shake of head before she came over to her and wrapped a hand around her arm and took her to the bathroom.

"You'll get a cold if you don't take a warm shower right now." Lauren knew what Scarlet had meant but a part of her mind couldn't help but to wander to an alternative place where Scarlet was helping her take her clothes off for that mentioned warm shower.

Shaking away the thoughts, Lauren nodded before placing both of her hands around herself. "Yeah, I'll just do that." She spoke awkwardly as she began to push Scarlet out of the bathroom.

Scarlet, nodded her head, and walked out of the bathroom but not before pointing out something to Lauren, "I can see that you don't like to wear a bra before sleep."

For a moment, Lauren stared at Scarlet's smirking face with confusion, before her own face turned a dark red and she slammed the door shut in Scarlet's face. Looking down at her now see through shirt, she slapped her forehead before taking it off, getting ready for a shower.

Scarlet, who was now standing staring at the bathroom door with wet clothes, sighed heavily before she smiled.

"Hurry up in there, okay. I also don't like wearing undergarments before sleep." Smirking at the little groan that came from inside, she was satisfied with herself.

"Tonight, you are a free man, my brother. But tomorrow, you're gonna be back to being Vanessa's fiancé." Scarlet came into the kitchen, hearing Blake's voice as he talked to Kevin.

"If you even think of sleeping around tonight, I'm going to cut you where the sun doesn't shine." Scarlet joined the two men's conversation, throwing a sickeningly sweet smile towards Kevin, who shivered in response. "I promise, I won't."

"Good boy." She commented as she filled a cup of coffee before raising the cup towards him and leaving the kitchen with one last glance thrown his way.

All the while, Blake sat on the sides, laughing behind his hand that was covering his mouth.

Tonight, was the two bachelor parties that were for Vanessa and Kevin. While the men would be going to a strip club which was going to be serving lots of food. The women were going to stay in.

The kids were going to be sent to sleep after 10, after which the party would start.

Juliet had still yet to tell anyone about her preparations for the bachelorette party, and as Scarlet entered the living room, she saw her sister sitting beside Juliet on the sofa, trying to get information out of her about tonight.

"Come on, just whisper it in my ear." Vanessa said as she brought her ear close to Juliet's mouth. Juliet, noticed Scarlet entering the living room, and sent her a look of help.

"Hey, Vanessa, try tickling her. Maybe she might break." Scarlet spoke and Juliet glared at her cousin before she tried to make a run for it. "Nuh uh, you are not running away without telling me about that party." Vanessa laughed before she began to tickle her younger cousin, who just began laughing uncontrollably while pleading Vanessa to stop, in between.

Satisfied of the outcome, Scarlet sat down on the recliner, placing her feet on the coffee table and drinking her cup of coffee in peace, while Vanessa tickled Juliet mercilessly.

"I will.... kill you." Juliet gasped in between laughs as she tried to escape from Vanessa's tickling fingers. "In your dreams." Scarlet laughed when Juliet fell from the sofa on her back, and groaned but was back to laughing when Vanessa moved from the sofa to the carpeted floor while still continuing her torture.

Lauren, who had just come downstairs, heard the laughter from the living room. Entering the living room, her eyes went to Scarlet first and foremost before they turned to Vanessa who was assaulting Juliet with tickles.

"Laur-ren, help!" Juliet laughed as she gave Lauren a pleading look. Scarlet shook her head before she got off the recliner and went over to Lauren. "No, don't help her. Let her suffer."

Vanessa laughed before she stopped her torture on her young cousin and looked at her sister instead. "Why the sudden coldness towards her?" Vanessa asked and Scarlet whined. "Why'd you let her go?"

Juliet stuck her tongue out to Scarlet before sitting up on the sofa.

"I dumped water on Lauren and her. It's not my fault they're so sickeningly sweet." Juliet answered Vanessa's question and Scarlet glared at her. "Yeah, also tell her about the part where I threatened you."

Juliet visibly shivered before awkwardly laughing, "What were they doing that was so sickeningly sweet?" Vanessa asked while chuckling, and this was the part where Scarlet and Juliet glanced at each other while Lauren stood awkwardly at the side lines, not wanting to be dragged into the current conversation.

"Just, stuff." Juliet answered and as Vanessa turned to her to give the said girl a frown, Scarlet face-palmed herself. "What she meant to say is that we were both cuddling because... of the slight cold last night."

Vanessa gave Scarlet a confused look before voicing out her thoughts, "Why didn't you just get a blanket?"

Scarlet began to sweat with nervousness as she gave Juliet a look, "That's a good question. Juliet will answer that." Juliet panicked when Vanessa looked at her, wanting an answer.

"I....I-I, actually, Lauren might know better." Lauren looked at the two cousins before smiling at Vanessa. "I hear my phone ringing."

Lauren lied as she gave the two cousins a glare, before escaping the questioning gaze of Vanessa and exiting the living room.

"I hear mom calling me." Scarlet spoke as she placed her hand behind her ear. "I should go before she comes down. You know how old she is getting, she cant afford to walk up and down the stairs for nonsense like this." Scarlet rambled with a nervous smile.

"I hear her calling me, too." Juliet nodded her head frantically as she lied and got off the sofa before speed-walking out of the living room. Scarlet smiled at her sister before leaving the living room as well, leaving Vanessa with a confused expression.

"What the hell just happened?" Vanessa spoke out aloud as she looked around the living room with confusion.

"And remember, don't let any woman touch you suggestively." Vanessa warned as she tied Kevin's tie, who nodded with a loving smile on his face as he took in Vanessa's frowning face. "You look really cute when you're jealous."

"I'm not jealous." Vanessa spoke as she brought her eyes to Kevin's face, away from the tie she had just tied. "And don't even give me a reason to be jealous, or else."

Kevin chuckled before pecking her lips, "I won't." Vanessa smiled before embracing him, "Good." She spoke into his chest as he stroked her hair.

"Oh, come on! He's not going to war! Let him go!" Blake shouted as he danced on the heels of his feet in front of the open front door. "Yeah. He's going to be a free man only once tonight. Let him be." Andrew spoke as he heartily laughed.

Vanessa glared at her cousin and father separately, before giving Kevin a look of pure warning. "If you thought dad and I were scary, wait till you get a load of Van-hell." Scarlet spoke as she leaned against the doorway of the living room with a bottle of cola in her hands.

"Thank you, Scarlet, for the heads up." Vanessa looked at Scarlet with an unimpressed look while Scarlet smiled sweetly at her sister. "My pleasure, Van-hell."

"Don't listen to her, baby. I'm not scary." Vanessa cooed in Kevin's ear as he smiled lovingly at her.

"Just wait." Scarlet spoke and got a nearby vase thrown at her, "Leave Scarlet."

"Dad, she threw a vase at me!" Scarlet complained as she grasped the weapon of assault in her hands. Andrew gave her a look before bursting out into laughter.

"You two are grown-ups. Solve your fights like grown-ups. Don't come to me about it." Scarlet opened her mouth in shock as she glared at her father.

"Well, we better go now or Kevin's gonna never want to leave." Blake sighed before he grabbed Kevin's arm and began to drag him out of the house.

"Be safe!" Vanessa yelled as Blake dragged Kevin to the car while Andrew walked out of the house, waving at his daughters.

"You too." Andrew winked as he went over to the car and a minute later, it was driving out of the driveway and disappearing down the road.

"Did that wink suggest something?" Vanessa turned to look at Scarlet with an unamused look. "Van-hell, huh?"

Scarlet laughed before running into the living room while Vanessa closed the door. "You better be ready for an attack, Scarlet!"

Inside the living room, the Payne women – Laura, Wanda and Judith – sat playing card games while Scarlet and Lauren were watching news on the t.v with a considerable amount of space between them.

Although, they kept glancing at each other and subtly touched each other's finger tips, they didn't move to get rid of it.

Juliet was upstairs, reportedly putting the children to sleep.

Vanessa walked in the living room and sat down beside Laura, with a sigh. "Cheer up, tonight's your bachelorette party too." Lauren spoke as she brought her knees to her chest while smiling at the woman.

"We don't even know what's going to happen." Scarlet mumbled sourly and got a slap on her arm from Lauren.

"Where is Juliet, by the way?" Judith asked as she looked at Scarlet, who shrugged in response. "She's up getting the kids to sleep." Vanessa spoke up before quieting down again.

"Yeah, like she'll ever get them sleep." Scarlet snorted and got a slap on the neck by Laura. "Don't be mean. Let her try."

Even when Laura knew that no one could control the little humans except for Scarlet, who had gotten the title of baby whisperer among the family, she was willing to let Juliet try.

"Why don't you go check on them?" Judith spoke as she gave Scarlet a nervous look. "You know how your cousin gets when she gets annoyed. I'm afraid she'll try to drug them to get them to sleep."

Scarlet laughed while Laura looked at Judith with her mouth wide open. She didn't say anything since Judith herself was doubtful of her own daughter.

Getting up from beside Lauren, Scarlet had just walked to the living room entrance when the doorbell rang. Looking back at the other ladies, Scarlet raised a questioning eyebrow at them, getting multiple shrugs in response from the women.

Shrugging, herself, Scarlet moved to the front door and opened the door wide open, coming face-to-face with three unknown men, who were wearing simple t-shirts and jeans.

One of them smiled at Scarlet before brushing his long locks of blonde hair back on his head, "Hi, I'm Dustin."

"And I'm Carl." The second one spoke while waving slightly at the dark-haired woman.

"Ben." The third one spoke in a bored tone.

"Um, do I know you?" Scarlet spoke as she gave the men a once over. They weren't awfully attractive, but attractive enough to be models. Hell, maybe they were models.

"Juliet.... Invited us?" Dustin spoke in a questioning tone as he looked at his companions. Carl nodded his head frantically while Ben just grunted. "Okay." Scarlet dragged out the word before side-stepping out of the way and letting the three men in.

"I'll just go....... bring her down." Scarlet spoke after she had guided the three men to the living room where the Payne women and Lauren, looked extremely confused.

Without any explanation to the women, Scarlet almost ran up the stairs and burst into the guest room. "Juliet." Her voice wasn't loud but it was loud enough to wake a person, and that person just happened to be Greg.

"You ding dong." Juliet hissed as Gregory began to whine and then jump into Juliet's lap, who was sitting on his mattress with a story book in her hands.

Scarlet noticed the awakening of Greg and just smiled apologetically at her cousin, "Sorry. Let me help."

She made her way over to her cousins and sat down beside Juliet before picking Greg up and placing him in her own lap. Looking around the room, she saw that the twins had fallen asleep while holding their hands – an old habit that didn't seem to go – and Greg was the only one that wasn't asleep.

"You have three handsome men downstairs, waiting for you." Scarlet informed the red-haired woman in a whisper before stroking Greg's hair, silently lulling him back to sleep.

At first, Juliet looked confused but then her confusion was replaced by panic and realization. "What?" She hissed in a whisper as she stood up almost immediately. Looking at the wall clock hanging just above the bathroom door, she cursed underneath her breath before sprinting out of the room, leaving Scarlet confused.

By now, Greg was fast asleep in Scarlet's arms, clutching lightly on to her shirt. She cooed at her adorable sleeping cousin before placing him back on the make-shift bed gently as to not to wake him up again before getting up from her sitting position.

Walking over to the light switch, she switched it off, letting the room engulf in darkness before walking out of the room, closing the door behind her with a soft click.

Scenarios were swirling in her head as to who those three men were as she began to descend downstairs. They could be anyone. Maybe Juliet's co-workers or maybe her old college mates. What confused Scarlet the most was the suspiciously identical attire of theirs which just brought many more questions into her head.

Scarlet's questions were to be answered eventually. Because the moment, she walked into the living room, she found the three men dancing up on Vanessa while she sat on the recliner completely enjoying the show they were putting.

The most mentally scarring part of the whole scene was the fact that they were now shirtless and their jeans were replaced with jean shorts.

Scarlet's reaction to all of this: Jaw on the floor.

Chapter 13

"What the hell is happening here?" Scarlet had managed to ask just after she recovered from her previous shock.

Lauren was the first one to even acknowledge the presence of the dark-haired girl, as she came over to Scarlet from the sofa where she was sitting, "Apparently, Juliet had male dancers invited." Scarlet shook her head with a frown.

"More like strippers." It was safe to say that Scarlet was really disturbed by the image that was now burned into her brain for her entire life time.

"Oh, let her just have fun." Lauren smiled as she watched how happy Vanessa looked when she had an excited Dustin giving her a lap dance while Ben and Carl were occupied with just dancing sexually around the recliner that was occupied by the Vanessa.

The coffee table was moved away from the center of the living room and was now placed against the farthest wall.

Vanessa was laughing maniacally while Juliet stood on the sidelines, watching her cousin's enjoyment. "Isn't this just fun!?"

She exclaimed as she looked at Vanessa with a huge grin on her face.

"Yes! This is so much fun! I love you, Juliet!" Vanessa exclaimed back with laughter still pouring out of her. Juliet smirked at Scarlet, who was watching from the doorway of the living room with her jaw dropped.

She raised her index finger before retrieving something from inside her jeans' pocket. "Here, use this." She handed a stack of dollar bills to her cousin. Vanessa looked at the stack before giving the other woman a meaningful look.

Juliet just nodded with a smirk before walking over to Scarlet, who was mentally damaged after all of this.

Vanessa had started being handsy as she tucked some dollar bills in Dustin's shorts while screaming occasionally with enjoyment.

"She looks so happy." Juliet stated as she smirked at Scarlet, who was ready to just burst out all of the things that were disturbing her in that moment.

Shaking her head, Scarlet tried to look at the bright side. At least, her grandmother wasn't a part of this. For once in her life, Scarlet was relieved that her grandmother loved to sleep or else, her mind would've something even more disturbing engraved in it. Certainly, seeing her grandmother be given a lap dance by half-naked young men was something on a completely different level than watching her sister be given one.

"Juliet, I need a really good reason not to punish you, young lady." Judith appeared in front of the three women as she glared at her daughter, and if looks could kill, Juliet would've been a dead woman by now. "Why mom? Look how happy Vanessa is." The slight whine in Juliet's voice wasn't hard to miss as Lauren raised an eyebrow at this.

Scarlet rolled her eyes as Judith turned to look at Vanessa, who was no doubt, enjoying the show the three men were putting. "Look how she's enjoying herself." Juliet added as she pointed her whole hand towards Vanessa's direction, who was now throwing money over the three men. "She's so happy. Do you want to punish me for making someone this happy?"

Lauren's jaw dropped when Judith's face held regret and she looked at her own daughter with pride. "No. Just. Don't let your grandmother see...... this." She spoke as she gestured to the three half-naked men.

"Uh-huh, I won't." Juliet's attitude took a 360 degree turn and she smiled brightly at her mother.

Judith nodded awkwardly before going back to, where she came from, maybe the kitchen.

"And that's how you get what you want." Juliet smirked. Lauren was only a second away from falling to her knees and asking the woman to teach her, her ways, but was snapped out of her awed state when Scarlet grabbed Lauren's arm.

"We are not going to watch men dance around. We – if you haven't noticed – are lesbians." Scarlet whispered harshly as to not let anyone else hear her besides Lauren and Juliet.

Juliet rolled her eyes before crossing her arms across her chest. Lauren, who had an awkward smile on her face, placed her other hand on top of Scarlet's bicep and leaned in to whisper in her ear. "Maybe we should stay." Scarlet jerked back a little to look at Lauren dumbfoundedly. "But they're half-naked." The emphasis on 'half-naked' was intended as Scarlet gave Lauren a confused look.

"Do you……. enjoy watching this?" Scarlet's eyes widened as she looked at Lauren, who smiled nervously. "Well, I never said that I was a complete lesbian." Lauren's voice was really low, but not low enough for Scarlet to not hear her.

Juliet's eyebrow raised as she looked back and forth between the two women, as if she expected a fight – a juicy informative fight.

"So, you're bisexual?" It was said as a question even when it was pretty certain what Lauren had implied. "Yes." Lauren's voice was small as if she was embarrassed to even admit that she liked men as well.

Scarlet stood unmoved for a moment as she kept staring at Lauren, before a frown graced her face and she – without a word being said – walked over to the sofa and sat down with a plop.

Juliet looked confused at her, "Is that a sign that you can stay too, or what?" Lauren didn't know that as well as she went over to sit next to the dark-haired woman.

"Lesbians are so confusing." Juliet mumbled to herself as she rolled her eyes at her cousin.

Ben smirked when he saw the blonde woman sitting on the sofa and without much delay stood in front of her, ready to give her an extremely sexual lap dance.

But his intentions were halted as a voice was heard from the entrance of the living room, and for a moment everything stopped. Vanessa looked past Dustin, to see the one and only grey-haired granny Payne, who didn't look the slightest bit of amused.

"What is happening here?" Her words came out strict and hard as she gave Vanessa a mean glare while Pudding was yipping away at the grey-haired woman's feet.

"It was Juliet's idea!" Vanessa quickly spoke as she pointed at Juliet, who immediately shook her head, denying Vanessa's claims. "I don't even know why Vanessa is lying." Vanessa glared at her younger cousin before pushing the man from in front of her.

Ben and Carl had immediately went to stand in the corner of the living room like guilty puppies, when they had heard Granny Payne's voice. Dustin glared at Vanessa before he joined his two companions, crossing his arms across his chest.

Scarlet was just moments away from running into the kitchen to prepare some popcorn for the current situation.

"I can't believe that you were having a party without me." Granny Payne complained as she walked into the living room completely, with Pudding following her closely.

As if, he had been given a bone, he ran over to Scarlet while yipping here and there. It was as if she was a dog whisperer as well.

Rolling her eyes, Scarlet shooed the dog away who had decided to just lay near her feet with his tongue falling out of his mouth. Lauren cooed silently at the sight.

Lauren didn't know if Scarlet was angry at her or not. Judging by the sour expression on Scarlet's face just because of Pudding, made her think otherwise. Maybe, Scarlet was mad at her for not telling her that she was bisexual.

It wasn't that Lauren wanted other men, it was just that she also liked them as much as she liked women. She did have two boyfriends, before she acknowledged her attraction towards women as well.

"Oh." Juliet smirked with an evil glint in her eyes as she looked at Granny Payne. "We're sorry for not inviting you, but you were sleeping, so we thought to not disturb you." Granny Payne's eyes turned to the red head that was giving her grandmother an apologetic look.

"Why don't we compensate for that?" Scarlet's ears twitched as she squinted her eyes at her cousin that did not seem to have good intentions at all.

Granny Payne's eyebrow rose as she gave her granddaughter a confused look. "You just have to sit here." Juliet was sure to throw Vanessa a look to leave the recliner immediately.

Smirking at her cousin, Vanessa quickly obliged and stood up from the recliner while Lauren looked back and forth between Juliet and Vanessa with confusion. Even though Lauren had no idea of Juliet's intentions, Scarlet was well aware as she shook her head to get rid of the thought of what Juliet might be doing.

Guiding Granny Payne towards the recliner, Juliet called Dustin over, with a wave of her hand.

Confused, Dustin came to the red head, who was now stood in front of her sitting grandmother. "Enjoy the show." Juliet smiled widely as Dustin understood and immediately went to work.

Scarlet face-palmed as Dustin began to give Granny Payne a lap dance, who was now looking frightened but still excited.

"Mom!" Scarlet yelled as she stood up, making the blonde sitting beside her flinch from the loudness of her voice. "Aunt Judith!"

A second later, the three women were walking into the living room with cups of coffee – which they had prepared because of their boredom. Upon stepping foot into the confines of the living room, Laura was the one that had dropped her cup on the carpeted floor on seeing Dustin dancing up on Granny Payne.

"Mother!" Judith and Wanda just had their jaws wide open as they watched the way Dustin's hips moved sexually over the old woman's lap.

It looked scandalous and dirty, and Granny Payne agreed 100%.

"I feel so scandalous and dirty!" Granny Payne yelled as she laughed crazily. Ben and Carl smirked at the way the old woman enjoyed herself before they locked their eye-sights on their targets.

Vanessa grinned at the way her grandmother enjoyed the show as she sat on the sofa beside Lauren, who was just utterly confused and embarrassed of what was happening now.

Laura and Wanda went to Granny Payne, to make Dustin stop his naughty dance, while Judith went over to her daughter to give her a lengthy lecture. Judith dragged Juliet to the kitchen where she was going to be sure to give her daughter an earful of nagging.

Scarlet glared at the retreating back of the red head as she crossed her arms across her chest. It was difficult enough for her to erase the image of her sister getting a lap dance from her memory and now she had just witnessed something even more disturbing and scarring.

And on top of that, she was completely displeased by the half-naked men. Speaking of half-naked men, she noticed that Ben and Carl were now occupied with Vanessa and Lauren.

Vanessa was looking quite entertained while Lauren didn't know what to do.

There were two reasons for that. First: she never had someone give her a lap dance and, second: Scarlet was in the room, which was a good enough reason on its own.

"Woah, buddy. It's not her bachelorette party." Scarlet's jealousy flared and she pulled Ben away from the blonde woman that looked back and forth from Scarlet and Ben.

"We were solely hired to give lap dances. It doesn't matter if she's the one getting married or not." Ben spoke with a smirk as he eyed Scarlet up and down slyly.

"Yeah, chill out, Scarlet." Vanessa spoke with a laugh as she spared Scarlet a glance. "Or maybe, you want him to give you a dance instead." The wink sent her way by Ben was even more disgusting than the idea of having been given a lap dance by a man.

"No thank you." Scarlet spoke quickly as she stepped a few inches away from Ben, who was giving her suggestive looks.

Lauren frowned as her imagination worked wonders and she imagined Ben straddling Scarlet, while grinding his crotch against her while she enjoyed.

Shaking her head to clear away the image that was now fully formed in her head, she frowned deeply. She couldn't let that happen even if it was quite unlikely for Scarlet to enjoy anything sexual from men.

Her hand moved on its own as she pulled on Ben's wrist and made him turn towards her instead of the dark-haired woman.

Scarlet looked in disbelief at Lauren, as she watched the way Ben gave Lauren a suggestive smile and Lauren smiled back at him lightly. Vanessa noticed the way Scarlet's eyes flashed anger and then hurt as she turned around to leave the living room without giving a second glance back. Raising an eyebrow at it, Vanessa couldn't help but to feel suspicious.

Lauren's eyes were trained on Scarlet as she watched her leave the living room and the only thing that was now left in her head was a single thought: 'What have I done?'

By now, Juliet was bored and utterly apologetic as her mother kept up her verbal assault. Juliet had apologized millions of times now and was just hoping for her mother to forgive her, or better yet, stop nagging.

Laura and Wanda were successful in getting Granny Payne away from the long-haired man that she was getting well-acquainted with.

"You should be ashamed of your conduct. You, not only brought male strippers in this house, but also got your grandmother involved in all of this." Juliet rolled her eyes at the repeated sentence. "I'm sorry, I'm really sorry, okay. What else do you want from me? I already apologized, a total of 24 times."

Judith glared at her daughter before turning away from her. "I'm seriously disappointed in you, young lady. I hope you have a better excuse to give to your father."

"I'm a grown woman now, mom." Juliet burst as she glared back at her mother. "I don't need you to tell on me to dad. He wouldn't have minded this anyway." The underlying message wasn't hard to miss as Judith stared wide-eyed at her daughter.

Judith didn't have anything else to say as Juliet walked out of the kitchen with heavy but quick steps.

Entering the living room again, Juliet noticed how Lauren sat looking miserable on the sofa beside an entertained Vanessa. The three men were back to only tending to Vanessa. Laura and Wanda had left the living room with Granny Payne, who was whining about going back to the living room.

"Party's over." Juliet announced as she clapped her hand once with a frown on her face. The three stopped and quickly straightened themselves up while picking up the pieces of their clothes that they had stripped out of.

As if noticing the absence of Scarlet, Juliet asked, "Where's Scarlet?"

Lauren looked at the red head before she quickly went out of the living room in search of the said woman.

Juliet watched Lauren with confusion until she was out of the living room before turning to the three – now fully clothed – men. They worked fast.

"Um, goodbye then." She spoke with awkwardness as she looked at the three. She had already paid them and was ready for them to leave. "Uh, we're sorry, you got in trouble because of us." Dustin spoke as he looked at Juliet with genuine concern on his face.

Juliet simply nodded before shrugging, "I get in trouble all the time."

When the three men were gone and Juliet had come back to the living room, where only Vanessa was sitting, she sighed heavily. "What a night, right?"

Vanessa stared at her cousin before she crossed her arms and spoke what was really on her mind, "What is going on between Scarlet and Lauren?"

Juliet looked at her cousin with wide eyes as she coughed nervously before shaking her head, "N-Nothing. Why would you ask?"

"I know that you're hiding something from me. There is something more to their relationship."

Juliet wasn't sure how Vanessa had found out about this but she was certain that she wouldn't get any information out of her.

"There is nothing more to their platonic relationship."

Vanessa didn't believe her.

Lauren knew where Scarlet would be, which led her straight to the rooftop where – undoubtedly – Scarlet was.

She was looking out into the wide spread darkness as a frown still graced her features, when Lauren took a seat beside her. The dark-haired woman had already sensed the blonde's presence from the strong scent of vanilla.

It wasn't even a minute into the silence when Scarlet spoke, "Do you know what bothers me more than the thought that you didn't tell me you were bisexual?"

Lauren gulped before she spoke with her voice shaky, "What?"

"That Katie is bisexual too." Scarlet turned to look into Lauren's eyes that were holding regret. "I'm not angry that you wanted Ben to......" she trailed off as she looked away from Lauren.

"I'm not even mad at you for enjoying the little show they put on. I'm just furious that when I'm trying so hard to forget about Katie, you just keep reminding me of her more than anything."

Lauren didn't know what to say as she stared at Scarlet's expressionless face. "What do you want me to do?" Lauren's voice was low and shaky as she spoke.

Scarlet turned to Lauren with an emotionless face, "Leave me alone."

Lauren was taken aback by what had just come out of the older woman's mouth as she stared at Scarlet with hurtful eyes, "What?"

"Just leave me alone."

"I'm sorry, Scar. I truly am. I didn't mean to make you so angry. But don't push me away." Lauren's eyes were filling with tears as she scooted close to Scarlet. "I'm not angry. I just don't....... want to see you for now."

Lauren's breath hitched when she heard what Scarlet had just uttered.

"I can't move on if you keep on reminding me of Katie."

Lauren's tears were now flowing freely as she stared at Scarlet, who had turned away from her and was back to staring out into the spread darkness.

With hesitancy, Lauren stood up from her sitting position and left the rooftop with hurried steps as her tears were still falling from her eyes.

She was grateful that no one had witnessed her like this as she went to the guest room. She didn't want to answer anyone's questions.

Scarlet sighed heavily before her breaths became labored and her eyes became wet with moisture.

She was crying and she was remembering Katie, after hurting Lauren. Surely, this was the lowest that she could go.

Chapter 14

Scarlet was like a hostile lioness at the moment, as she roamed the house aimlessly, destroying her health with tons of Cola. Turns out that this was her way of coping with hurt.

While on the other side of her, Lauren was doing her very best in leaving Scarlet alone. She was even thoughtful in not even showing the dark-haired, her face. This was Lauren's way of coping.

And on the sidelines, Juliet and Blake were confused as to what occurred between the two that brought this much distance in-between them.

Before last night, they were finding it hard to even stay a few inches apart from each other, and now here they were, trying hard to maintain distance.

According to Blake, the bachelor party was wonderful and everyone had fun. And according to Juliet and the rest of the Payne women, the bachelorette party only consisted of 'board games and empowering women songs'.

"So, you guys just listened to Beyoncé and Spice girls?" Blake asked as he arched an eyebrow for special effect. "Yes." Juliet sipped her coffee as she stared at Lauren from across the dining room table, who was swirling a fork around her fried eggs.

"All night long?" Blake asked in disbelief as he took a bite of his toast. "Mmhm. A whole night of Beyoncé and Spice Girls, who runs the world?"

"Sweet." Juliet rolled her eyes at her simple-minded cousin.

"And so, what happened in lover's paradise?" Blake brought his voice to a low volume as he spoke in Juliet's ear.

The red head shrugged as she kept staring at the blonde woman play with her breakfast.

The Payne family members were all asleep and the only ones awake in the whole house were Blake, Juliet, Lauren and Scarlet, and one of them was busy wandering around the house while drowning herself in a certain dark brown liquid.

"I have no idea." Juliet muttered as she took another sip of her coffee. Lauren, who had a certain dark-haired woman on her mind, had lost her appetite after frying the eggs.

And now, she was just playing around with them, hoping for them to disappear themselves from her line of sight.

"Are you gonna eat that?" Lauren was brought out of her thoughts as she looked up at Blake, who was glancing from the fried eggs to the blonde woman. For a moment, she was confused as to what he had implied, but then her brain began to work properly.

"Yeah, sure." She pushed the plate towards Blake, who smiled gratefully at the blonde.

"Hog." Juliet muttered as she rolled her eyes.

Blake had chosen to ignore Juliet's remarks as he began to eat Lauren's breakfast. "I need some air." Lauren spoke abruptly as she stood up from the chair and turned to walk out the kitchen door frame.

At the door, she halted her steps as she watched the person on her mind descending from the stairs. Scarlet saw the way Lauren's face left all color and she quickly turned 180 degrees and walked the other way.

"I'll just walk in the backyard then." The blonde muttered under her breath as she changed her route and went over to the glass door separating the kitchen from the backyard.

When she had completely left the kitchen, Scarlet entered with two empty Cola bottles and a sour expression. "Morning." She grunted as she noticed her two favorite cousins sitting at the dinner table.

"Uh, morning." Blake grunted back with a sly smile while Juliet giggled. Scarlet could only manage to roll her eyes as she went over to the fridge to get some more Cola. Her eyes trailed to the backyard door through which she could see the blonde woman pacing around but she quickly averted her eyes as to not seem like a creep.

Scarlet was sure to stock her fridge with the beverage just after she had told Lauren to 'piss off' in cleaner words. What mostly made Scarlet regret ever saying that was the fact that Lauren was sure to obey her demand.

Even Katie wasn't this nice to just give Scarlet some space. She would've called or texted her until Scarlet caved in. One of the reasons why Scarlet had to change her number before coming back to her hometown.

Katie had texted her and left her millions of messages consisting of the same word repeated over and over with different sentence construction: Sorry.

It had pissed Scarlet off on a completely different level how Katie had believed that she could just make everything better with one word. One stupid overused, word.

"Good morning." Vanessa entered into the kitchen with her hair falling all over the place, causing Scarlet to snap out of her thoughts.

"Morning." Scarlet grunted again and Vanessa looked at her sister for a minute while Juliet and Blake observed from the table, like bystanders.

Juliet had told Blake what Vanessa had asked and she had even warned her older cousin that if Vanessa ever came to him with questions relating Scarlet or Lauren, he was to lie and deny anything that was true.

"You seem to be in a bad mood." Vanessa spoke as she went to get some coffee, that Juliet had prepared. "I could say the same to you." Scarlet gave Vanessa a once over and smirked with her eyes showing nothing but hollowness. Grabbing a bottle of her favorite liquid, she shut the fridge's door and leaned against it.

"Feeling sick?" For a second, Vanessa, had widened her eyes but then she nodded her head reluctantly. "Yeah, just morning sickness. You know."

"Yeah." Scarlet nodded. Blake and Juliet glanced at each other before they stood up from their seats.

"Well, we better go. It's a long day ahead of us." Blake smiled at his two cousins while Juliet just tried to not meet their eyes and leave the kitchen without getting called out by them.

Vanessa squinted her eyes at the red head before she turned back to her sister, who was gulping down the brown liquid without any remorse.

"You look pitiful." Scarlet glared at her sister as she brought the bottle away from her mouth. "You look annoying as ever, am I complaining?"

Vanessa managed to roll her eyes before her eyes strayed to Lauren, who could be visibly seen from the glass backyard door. "What's up between you and Lauren?"

Scarlet just smiled sarcastically, "Nothing."

With squinted eyes, Vanessa shook her head, "I know there's something more to your relationship with her, than you lead on."

"What if there is? What are you gonna do, go tell on me to mom and dad, since that's what you've always done before?" Vanessa's mouth dropped open as she watched the way Scarlet opened the fridge again and grabbed two more bottles of cola, before leaving the kitchen without anything else said.

Vanessa couldn't help but to bring her eyes back to the blonde that was pacing around in the backyard aimlessly.

She knew that something was going on between the two and she couldn't help but to find out what. Since, she had always thought that Scarlet having unexplained crushes on women was just a phase.

Unbeknownst to her, it wasn't.

No one had known how this had happened to be as Vanessa drove the car while Lauren sat awkwardly on the passenger's seat. There was no music, no noise and definitely no talking.

Even the car's own noises were not enough to cut through this thick awkward silence as Lauren stole subtle glances at the woman beside her.

The two women had come to this, when Vanessa asked her mother if she could go to the flower shop instead of her, and decide on the flowers for the flower arrangements herself.

Laura had happily agreed on it.

Lauren had just been minding her own business, and by that, I mean, she was just trying extremely hard to not let Scarlet even get a glance of her face, when Vanessa had told her to come with.

Completely confused, Lauren tried to get out of it but then Laura made her go with the almost bride-to-be.

"I'm sure, we'll find some great flowers." Vanessa had said to Lauren as they had just stepped out of the house with the essential things; money, car keys and pepper spray.

Lauren had just managed to nod her head slowly as she followed the other woman quickly towards her car.

And now, that they were sitting in thick silence and Vanessa was being extra-ordinarily picky with choosing which flower shop she wanted her flower arrangements from, Lauren realized that this was going to take a whole lot of time.

A part of her was happy that she would be able to not run into Scarlet if she wasn't even in the house, but another part of her was already missing Scarlet. Even though, they had only been affectionate for a small amount of time, she was already addicted to the small kisses and cuddles.

"So, what do you do?" Vanessa broke Lauren away from her thoughts, as she glanced at her while driving. Lauren, at first, didn't know why she was even been asked that question but then she realized that the older woman was trying to make small talk.

"Oh, I'm a model." Vanessa's eyebrow raised as she had to glance at Lauren another time, while Lauren only gave her a small smile. "What work do you do?" Lauren asked back as she tried to loosen up her body. She was being extremely stiff.

"I'm a lawyer." It was hard for Lauren to not feel intimidated by Vanessa when she found out that the woman was a lawyer.

"Scarlet also wanted to pursue a career in law." Lauren turned her head to look at Vanessa with surprise. "Then how come she became a magazine editor instead?"

Vanessa glanced at the blonde woman before she sighed, "She's really stubborn, you know." Lauren's expression only showed confusion as Vanessa didn't exactly answer her question. "She likes to have power over her decisions. Over the things that concern her and that's the only reason why she didn't pursue law."

Lauren only nodded as she was still quite confused. "How about that shop over there?" The blonde immediately looked at the way that the other woman was pointing where a moderately sized flower shop stood with a sign above it saying 'Have A Flower' in italics.

Vanessa parked the car just in front of the small shop as she turned to Lauren, who was busy giving a once over to the shop which was literally overflowing with flowers.

"Scarlet loves flowers." It was a random piece of information about the girl but it was information nonetheless, and when Lauren turned to look back at Vanessa with her eyes twinkling, Vanessa could only manage to smile a wide fake smile.

The blonde younger woman was the first one to get out of the car while Vanessa took her time as she locked the car and then joined Lauren on the curb.

"Are we going to enter or not?" Vanessa asked when the blonde didn't proceed to take a step towards the shop.

Lauren, as if broken out of thought, nodded her head and began to walk towards the glass door of the shop. Opening it, the bell rang above it, notifying the owner that they had customers.

Looking around the space of the flower shop which was filled up to the brim with fresh smelling flowers, Lauren couldn't help but wonder which flower Scarlet loved the most.

Maybe she could gift her one, for an apology or for something that Lauren wasn't even sure of.

"Ah, girls with lovers, I presume." Lauren and Vanessa jumped as they turned their heads to look at the grey-haired woman that had appeared out of nowhere. Well, not out of nowhere, but just out of someplace that the two women didn't know or notice.

Lauren blushed deeply while Vanessa smiled widely – this time genuinely – as she nodded her head happily. "I'm going to get married next week."

The blonde felt a little bitter as she looked at the wide smile and the sparkling eyes of the almost bride. She wondered how it would feel like to be this happy, to be marrying the one person that she really loved. But with wondering about happiness, all she could get reminded of was a certain brown-haired unemployed woman.

"Congratulations, dear," the old woman smiled back at Vanessa before her eyes trailed to the blonde, "and what about you, pretty girl?"

For a minute, Lauren stood unmoving before she smiled nervously," I don't have a lover."

"Nonsense, I can see it in your eyes that you have someone that you love deeply."

As Lauren looked at the old woman incredulously, she thought to herself, 'Are my eyes that obvious?'

She was only a moment away from touching her eyes but controlled herself as she shook her head, lying, "I don't have anyone."

Besides, all she could do was lie. Vanessa was there and she would find out if she told the old woman about Scarlet.

The slight raised eyebrow of the woman told Lauren that she did not believe her as she moved on away from her and to the soon-to-be-bride.

"So, what can I help you with, dear?"

Vanessa, clearing away her thoughts, spoke excitedly, "I need flower arrangements for my wedding."

"Oh, Forget-me-nots and Red Roses would suit your wonderful day best," The old woman spoke as she plucked a rose and a forget-me-not from somewhere behind her, "Forget-me-nots symbolize the bond between two people lasting for eternity to come. While, the rose is a great sign of love, as you already might know."

Vanessa's eyes were wide with wonder and awe as she looked at the forget-me-not. "They're beautiful."

"And for you, dear," The grey-haired woman turned around again to fumble with the flowers before finding what she needed, "A Hydrangea and Gardenia."

Lauren glanced at Vanessa, who shrugged her shoulders while the old woman held out the two flowers out to the blonde.

"What do these two mean?" Vanessa asked as her curiosity got the best of her.

The old woman looked at Lauren for a moment too long before she turned completely to the brown-haired woman. "Shall we, instead, talk about the arrangements of the flowers at your wedding, my dear?"

The way that Vanessa's eyes lit up, was proof enough at how she had completely forgotten about the two flowers that Lauren now held in her hands.

"I want the roses at the entrance while...." Vanessa began to talk animatedly as she smiled widely at every word while Lauren was left to wonder what the two flowers meant and why did the old lady give them to her.

When it was time for them to say farewell to the old lady, Vanessa produced a large sum from her jeans' pocket that Lauren was unaware of, which the old lady declined to take before the work had already been done.

Vanessa told the woman about the venue and all the little details while Lauren held on tightly to the two flowers.

"Take care now, dear." The old lady waved as Vanessa walked out of the shop with a single rose and forget-me-not in hand, which was free of cost and gifted to her by the old woman.

"Um, if you don't mind me asking. Then can you please tell me what do these flowers mean?" Lauren asked when she saw that Vanessa was in the car and still dazed from her excited talk with the flower lady.

The old woman smirked which looked almost like a smile as her cheeks were hanging slightly. "You should know better since these two can easily explain your state in two words."

"I don't understand what you're saying." Lauren spoke firmly as she held her ground with a frown on her face.

The old woman gave the blonde woman a smile now, as she began, "A hydrangea symbolizes heartfelt emotions and also expresses gratitude for being understood," The smile on the woman's face stayed as she saw the blonde's frown deepen.

"Ah, and the Gardenia represents secret love."

Lauren's eyes were unable to open more than they were now open as she stared at the old woman with a scared look.

"Don't worry, dear. Some people need flowers to convey their feelings and that is why, the Hydrangea is just for you and your secret lover."

The wink sent her way, made Lauren smile slightly as she looked down at the two flowers she held in the palm of her hand.

"Thank you."

"No need, dear. I'm just an old lady that's obsessed with flowers and feelings."

The silence in the car was back to being awkward as the two women sat silently, not uttering a single word to one another.

"So, what do these flower mean?" Vanessa broke the heavy silence as she glanced down at the two flowers that were – now – in Lauren's lap.

"Uh, they just mean heartfelt emotions." Lauren half-lied as she nervously chuckled. Vanessa nodded before she glanced at Lauren.

"Then do they represent your feelings for Scarlet?"

Lauren was going to say yes but then she was reminded of who she was talking to and she quickly shook her head. "N-no. They don't."

The sudden jerk of the car stopping, scared Lauren more than she was when Scarlet had told her nicely to fuck off.

"Don't play games with me." Vanessa's voice could be identified as a killer's as she turned herself completely towards the blonde – scared – woman.

"I don't understand w-what you're talking about."

"I don't like you Lauren." The blonde was frightened of Vanessa's behavior as she sat rooted to her seat when all the instructions, of her brain was to open the car door and run away from the older woman.

"W-why?" Lauren managed to ask as she looked into Vanessa's eyes that were blazing. "Because I can see that you're trying to seduce Scarlet."

Lauren's mouth flew open as she stared at Vanessa in disbelief. Yes, Lauren wanted to seduce Scarlet but she wasn't doing it. Not that she was aware of, anyway.

"What? I'm not trying to seduce anyone."

"Oh yeah, then why do you two cuddle and steal glances of each other when no one's watching?" Vanessa's eyebrows moved up and down and she crossed her arms over her chest.

"What? We don't do that." Even Vanessa could tell the lie from Lauren's face, as the blonde nervously waved her hand dismissively while chuckling. "You and Kevin do that."

Vanessa rolled her eyes before she suddenly turned serious, "I know that Scarlet used to have crushes on girls but she outgrew that phase. But, now with you, I don't want her to go through that phase again."

Lauren wanted to do nothing more than to roll her eyes before screaming in Vanessa's face how wrong she was and how liking girls in a romantic way is never a phase but a sexuality and, there's a difference between the two.

"I don't know what you're saying, but don't you think that she's old enough to live her own life her own way." Lauren tried to keep her voice as neutral as possible but the venom just seeped through.

"I'm her older sister. So, to see, if her decisions are good enough for her, will always be my responsibility."

This time Lauren did roll her eyes as she stared at Vanessa, "It's her life!"

"I don't think you clearly understand how things in our family go, but the older people are always responsible for the younger ones and Scarlet, she's my sister. My younger sister, that I want to protect."

"From what?"

"From you!" Lauren backed up as she stared in Vanessa's eyes as they blazed with fury. "From being sick again!"

"Please, take me home." Lauren crossed her arms as she leaned back in her seat with a frown gracing her lips. "It isn't your home." And with that Vanessa started the car again, leaving Lauren with dark thoughts that weren't helping her current situations.

"What's crawled up her ass and died?" Blake asked Lauren, who wasn't in the best mood either. "I don't know, go ask her yourself."

"Woah, harsh." Lauren simply rolled her eyes and went upstairs as well with her flowers, where the other woman had gone off to as well.

The moment the two had entered the house, after Blake had opened the door, they only glared at each other. Vanessa, who was – as she said – tired, went up to her room to rest, while Lauren stayed only for a minute and in that minute, Blake managed to drive her away to the guest room as well.

Entering the room, Lauren noticed many things, like how the window was open and how the only person in the room was a sad looking Scarlet, and the empty glass bottles sat by her feet as she looked out of the window sitting on its pane.

Lauren wanted to leave without getting noticed but she couldn't do so when Scarlet brought all of her attention to the blonde.

"I'm sorry. I'll just leave." Lauren muttered quietly as she tried to not look into Scarlet's eyes because she knew that she would just break down if she looked into those eyes now. Her head was already filled with haunting thoughts of how she didn't belong here.

When she heard nothing back, she turned around and was about to walk out of the door again when she felt her hand being pulled back. "No, stay."

And Lauren did, without looking back, that is.

The silence was deafening as Lauren shifted her feet while her hand was still held by Scarlet's, who just stood staring at the ground.

"I'm sorry, I'm such a bitch." Scarlet spoke in a whisper as the silence surrounded them. "No, you're not."

"I am." Scarlet spoke firmly as she gripped Lauren's hand a bit tightly.

Lauren only winced whilst shaking her head frantically. "You're not."

"Why don't you look at me and say that, then?"

Scarlet's voice was low and ashamed as her hand began to shake before it dropped from Lauren's, but the blonde held it back as she turned around and looked up into the brown-haired woman's eyes.

"You're not."

Scarlet's eyes watered as she dropped her head onto Lauren's shoulder, "You're just saying that. I know, I hurt you."

"Yes, you hurt me but I hurt you too." Lauren pointed out as she brought her hand up to Scarlet's hair before she began to stroke her there. "I'm sorry for that."

"You shouldn't be. I'm sorry."

"No, I'm sorry."

"Lauren," Scarlet groaned as she brought her head up to look at her in her green eyes, "I am sorry."

"Shut up." Lauren rolled her eyes before pushing her back. "You're still mad at me." Scarlet's face turned sad again as she stared at the blonde.

"No, no. I was only joking." Lauren embraced the older woman as she nuzzled into her shoulder while Scarlet sighed heavily.

As if remembering the flowers in her hands now, Lauren excitedly gave the Hydrangea to Scarlet. "Here, this is for you."

"I thought about how to give it to you and all I could think of was to place it on your pillow but you were already here." Lauren rambled animatedly before taking a deep breath, making Scarlet chuckle at her.

"Oh, a beautiful flower." Scarlet studied the blue colored flower.

"Ask me what it means." Lauren giggled when Scarlet raised an eyebrow. "What does it mean?"

"I won't tell you." Lauren laughed in Scarlet's face before bringing her index finger to her lips, "It's a secret."

"Then why'd you make me ask you?" Scarlet groaned as she rolled her eyes. "Because."

"Yes, because?" Scarlet groaned once again in annoyance, "Because this flower represents my feelings."

"And you're feelings are?" Raising a single eyebrow, Scarlet crossed her arms while holding on to the flower that Lauren had just handed her.

"How about this?" Lauren spoke as a mischievous smirk played on her lips, "I'll tell you what it means if you kiss me."

Scarlet was more than okay with kissing the blonde as she pulled the woman closer to her by her waist before planting her lips onto the blonde's.

"It represents my heartfelt emotions." It was a whisper against her lips as Lauren closed her eyes to feel the moment, instead of just seeing it.

"And they are?" An involuntary eyebrow rose as Scarlet stared at the younger woman in front of her.

"You already know."

"I do, but you say it so sweetly." Lauren's lips curved as an involuntary smile came on to her face, while her dark thoughts faded away from her mind.

"I like you." Scarlet smirked when Lauren opened her eyes to look into her own. "Those are not your heartfelt emotions for me."

Lauren frowned as she stepped backwards to stare at Scarlet with confusion, "Yes, they are."

"No, you feel something much deeper for me than that." The way Lauren's face turned dark red made it obvious that it was the truth.

"I-I......" But before Lauren could stutter her way out of the current holds of Scarlet, she found herself being embraced in a hug, as Scarlet kissed under her ear. "No matter, you can say it when you're ready."

"The same way I'll say it when I'm ready." Lauren knew that Scarlet's words were truthful since she could feel the wildly beating heart of the older woman, while hers was beating in the same way. Fast and wild.

Both, with a flower each in one hand, embraced each other for a good amount of time. Just wanting to feel each other's hearts and body warmth, after staying away from each other for more than 16 hours.

One can't stay away from someone they love for too long.

****

Ta-da. Everything's good now. XD

For the people that celebrate christmas, I wish you the best and present to you this chapter that I wanted to update next week. So, to the devoted readers, this may be your present under the christmas tree (just kidding XD).

Have a great christmas and enjoy every part of it.

Vote if you like or comment but be sure to smile and carry on. XD

Chapter 15

With only a couple of days left till the wedding, Vanessa had been feeling quite nervous and the waves of morning sickness was brutal to a certain extent, where everyone had begun to wonder why she had started vomiting every morning and sometimes after eating.

Lauren had an idea and that came from the time when she had seen Vanessa coming into the house with a pregnancy box not so well hidden inside her purse.

A little of it peeked out and that little bit of it was enough for suspicions to arise inside of the blonde.

Now, the only thing that Lauren wanted to know was if the soon-to-be-bride was actually pregnant or just cautious.

On another room of the Payne household, there was Judith and Tyler, who were acting like it was the first time they had taken time to look at each other in the midst of all the preparations going on in the house.

"The Anderson's are going to come around today." Tyler spoke to his wife, who just nodded her head as she folded clean laundry.

"I know."

Tyler nodded his own head in acknowledgement before he looked up at his wife, who was still busy with what she was doing not far away from him.

Tyler was sat on their temporary bed as he looked at his wife work.

"I'm sorry about...."

"You don't have to apologize to me, apologize to Juliet." Judith cut him off while giving him an unforgiving glance. "I don't need your sorry-s."

Tyler sighed before rubbing his forehead, "I didn't know that she would see me."

"You should have told her everything from the very beginning. This...." Judith paused as she used her hands to gesture between the two of them, "....... this was sacred to her, and now it's just full of lies."

"Judith." Tyler sighed again as he looked at his wife with a defeated expression. "What can I do to make things better again?" His tone could almost show how defeated and torn he was, while his face told it completely.

"You......" Judith had nothing to say to him, nothing that was useful anyway. She wanted to curse him out, slap him a few times and maybe even expose him to the rest of the family, but the love that she felt in her heart for him was just too strong to let anything negative take control over her. "Just talk to Juliet."

Tyler nodded his head before he got off from the bed hesitantly, "You know that I still love you, right?"

Judith didn't meet his eyes as he stared at her and when he sighed after a minute, and walked towards the door to leave, only a small voice halted his steps. "I know."

"Do you think it's such a great idea?" Kevin asked as he snuggled closer into Vanessa's back as he tightened his arms around her body.

Vanessa sighed as she nodded her head, "It's necessary."

"Won't Scarlet be mad? I don't like her when she's mad, she's scary." Kevin shuddered, remembering how Scarlet had threatened him on the day of his bachelor's party.

"She will be for a while but then everything will work out. Besides, she needs to suck it up."

"Wow, that's harsh." Vanessa rolled her eyes before turning in Kevin's arms. "Would you like it better if she starts having unnatural thoughts again?"

Kevin looked into his fiancé's eyes and saw the slight fear and the concern, before he sighed, "If you think everything'll work out than it will."

Even when Kevin had an idea, that Scarlet felt something for Lauren already, he was torn in between the two women. To choose Vanessa's side or Scarlet's happiness.

For a man in love, he'd always side with the woman that means most to him. And to him, Vanessa was everything.

Vanessa nodded her head, pushing her body closer to Kevin's, wondering if what she was about to do was even worth it all. Her head was finding it logical and a good enough reason to be done, but her heart was finding it hard to agree on.

Scarlet was sitting beside an asleep Lauren, as she watched her closely. Blake and Juliet were out of the house, getting the wedding invitations that hadn't been handed out yet to anyone.

Greg was with Granny Payne, playing 'ladders and snakes', while the twins – Ed and Ed – were in the back yard with Pudding, since he hadn't been out of the house for quite some time.

The older woman brushed a strand of hair away from the blonde's closed eye as she smiled when the younger woman groaned softly before snoring lightly.

For Scarlet, watching Lauren came almost natural since the blonde's peaceful face brought peace to her as well. A peace that she couldn't explain or even find in anything else.

Lauren was beautiful.

And it wasn't even up for question.

Scarlet had known, since the day they had first met, the beauty that this blonde woman held in herself that no other could.

No doubt, Katie was also beautiful. Is beautiful, but she wasn't romantically beautiful to Scarlet anymore.

The type of beautiful that only your lover can be. Lauren was beginning to be that beautiful, and it was almost unfair, the way that Scarlet had found herself being sucked into that beauty and becoming something beautiful as well.

Not to herself, but definitely to Lauren, who couldn't put into words, the love she had begun to feel for the woman.

Lauren could see Scarlet's beauty, that was sharp-edged and sometimes stubborn but it was beauty nonetheless.

As Lauren shifted in her sleep, onto her side where Scarlet sat, she sighed out in relief when the older woman laid down.

Placing her arm around the blonde woman, Scarlet smiled as she watched Lauren breathing softly again.

"You should know that you're special." Scarlet spoke softly as she stroked Lauren's arm while laying on her back, "I never lay in bed in the middle of the day."

Lauren sighed as if she was awake and Scarlet looked down at her face to inspect if she was in fact asleep or not. When Lauren's breathing stayed soft and calm, she continued, "You're really special, Lauren."

Scarlet breathed in deeply before she tried to put herself to sleep in the arms of the woman that was already deep in her dreams.

"Okay, this one is going to my friends." Blake held up one of the invitation cards as he waved it around in the air, making Jared sigh out aloud.

"Boy, you better not invite some idiots to this wedding." Blake pouted as he looked at his father. "Hey, hey, hey, it's not his fault that he's an idiot and almost always finds other idiots to be his friends."

Blake's pout disappeared as he turned his head to glare at Scarlet, who was stood in the entrance of the living room. The woman stuck her tongue out at him, which only made Jared laugh at his son and niece.

"Don't gang up on my little Blake-y." Wanda came to the rescue as she literally hugged Blake's head, making the said boy to whine out at her. "Mom! Please don't ever call me 'Blake-y' again."

Wanda winked before leaving to go to the kitchen.

The whole family was piled up into the living room as they settled on who and where the wedding invitations would go.

The Anderson's weren't here yet and Scarlet was grateful for that. Even a single moment of peace was extremely appreciated. Kevin, the Anderson son, on the other hand, was seated next to Vanessa, while trying to figure out who he wanted to invite and who not to.

"Blake-y." Ed and Ed snickered while Juliet was slapping her knee, doubling over in laughter.

The twins were sitting on the carpet with Juliet and Greg, while Blake was sat beside on the other side of Vanessa on the couch. The recliner was occupied with Jared, and Granny Payne was on the sofa with Tyler and Andrew.

Wanda, Laura, and Judith had gone into the kitchen to make some snacks when Blake had brought in the two piles of invitation cards into the living room with Juliet trailing behind him with a satisfied smirk lighting up her face.

The first thing that had come out of Blake's mouth just after almost throwing the cards onto the coffee table was: "Damn, I never knew paper could even be this heavy."

The second: "Is this even paper?" As he looked at Juliet with a questioning look on his face.

Juliet had just shaken her head in pity before leaving the living room to call her whole family to the place.

Vanessa sighed in annoyance when the doorbell rang, already knowing who it was.

"I'll get it!" Lauren called out just as she came down the stairs and went towards the front door.

Opening the door, she faced the couple that was sporting happy smiles and a box of donuts.

"Ah, Lauren, wasn't it?" Mr. Anderson smiled as he handed the blonde the donuts box.

Lauren nodded as she held the box in her hands, giving the two a smile back. "I hope we aren't too late." Mrs. Anderson spoke worriedly as she looked at the blonde, who only shook her head and stepped aside for the two to enter.

"I'll go get these on a plate." Lauren spoke as she closed the door behind the couple, guiding them towards the living room.

"Hey, the Anderson's are here!" The living room came alive more than before as the couple entered the living room with smiles and hearty laughter.

Lauren shook her head with a smile before going to the kitchen to put the donuts on a plate before serving them.

The blonde woman had entered the kitchen just as the three women had left to go greet the Anderson's.

Placing the box down on the kitchen counter, Lauren got a plate that would be large enough to contain the donuts that were as many as the people in the house at the moment.

"Those look quite delicious." Lauren's eyes moved away from the plate to the older woman that stood in the doorway of the kitchen.

"Wait for them in the living room, then." Scarlet pouted as Lauren playfully rolled her eyes, while opening up the box before removing the donuts from the box and into the plate. "I should get a bonus for being your girlfriend."

Lauren's hand halted as she just took in the word. It wasn't as if Lauren had not considered the idea of being called Scarlet's girlfriend but being called that by the woman herself was far from her imagination.

"What did you say?" Lauren asked as she trained her eyes on the woman that was now looking at the blonde with a confused face. "What?"

"You just said the word 'girlfriend'."

"Yeah, so." Scarlet shrugged unknowingly as Lauren stared at her in disbelief. "I didn't know that we were girlfriends now."

"Well, we are, so you just have to deal with it." Scarlet smirked as she stared at Lauren seriously yet still amused. "Do I have a choice?" Lauren asked as her attention went back to her task at hand.

"No."

"That's what I thought." Scarlet chuckled as Lauren smiled to herself. "Can I have a donut now?"

The blonde looked back up at the dark-haired woman who was grinning childishly, in the doorway, before she shook her head. "No."

"That's what I thought."

This time, Lauren giggled while Scarlet left the kitchen doorway with a smile on her face even though she was denied a donut.

In the living room, only chattering could be heard. The overlapping of voices over each other's and how the only distinct voice was of Pudding, who would bark almost every 5 seconds.

Scarlet entered the kitchen and contemplated the idea of going back to the blonde, who was in the safety of the kitchen alone.

"Scarlet, tell Greg to stop calling me Blake-y." Blake whined from the sofa as Juliet smirked while patting Greg's head as if he was an obedient dog.

Scarlet sighed as she made her way over there, and sat down beside Juliet before pulling Greg towards herself. Juliet glared at her older cousin as she crossed her arms and mumbled about how she had ruined the fun for her.

Vanessa and Kevin were still deciding on the sofa about who to invite from California. There wasn't a lot of people there that they were friends with. Kevin had only a handful of friends that were also his acquaintances, while Vanessa had to decide from her whole firm on who to invite.

In the end, she decided to invite her boss and a few nice acquaintances, while Kevin chose to invite all of his friends.

"Do you want to invite anyone?" It was a question regarding Scarlet, who at first, looked pained before she composed herself and shook her head at her mother. Laura took her painful look as a sign that she missed Stewart. Oh, if only she knew the truth.

"Oh, Oh, wait! I have one more person to invite!" Kevin exclaimed as he looked at Blake, who was responsible of making the list and then getting the invitations delivered. "Who is it?" Kevin glanced at Vanessa, who suddenly realized something.

"Someone in New York." As if, she had been electrocuted harshly, her ears stood in attention and Scarlet turned her head to her sister and soon to be brother-in-law.

"But who do you want to invite in New York? You haven't even been there once in your life, honey." Mrs. Anderson questioned her son with clear confusion on her face.

Kevin smiled nervously before he nodded his head reluctantly, maybe thinking up a lie to feed his mother, "I had a friend in Cali move to New York, recently. I wanted to invite him."

Both of his parents nodded in understanding as did most of the Payne family, but something inside of Scarlet nagged her to not believe him and doubt him and that, she did.

"What's his name?" She asked just as the family went back to listing off the people they wanted to invite. "Huh?"

"What is your friend's name?" Kevin sat speechless as he glanced at Vanessa subtly before clearing his throat. "Sam. It's Sam."

Scarlet only managed to nod as she squinted her eyes at the man, who shifted fearfully under her scrutinizing stare.

"Who wants donuts?" In that exact moment, Lauren decided to appear in the semi-tense environment of the living room, where Scarlet was drilling holes into Kevin's head with her stare while Vanessa sat unaffected by it all, just beside Kevin, who was trying hard to not just cower into Vanessa's side.

"Ooh, us." The twins spoke in unison as they raised their hands together as well. Lauren chuckled at them before she came to place the plate full of donuts on the table which was half filled with invitation cards.

Granny Payne nudged Andrew as she pouted at him, the way a six-year-old girl would. Andrew stared at his mother for a while before he sighed defeatedly, "Blake, get your grandmother half a donut."

A triumphant smile came over the old woman's face as she beamed at his son before snatching away the half donut from Blake's outstretched hand.

On the other side of the living room, Lauren sat down beside Scarlet, getting a smile from the said woman and a frown from Vanessa.

"Why were you staring at Kevin like that?" Lauren whispered in Scarlet's ear, who shrugged as if to tell her to let it go. Juliet leaned in towards them and spoke in the same volume as Lauren, "Because Kevin has a friend in New York named Sam."

Lauren tilted her head to the side in confusion, making Scarlet almost coo at her and then peck her lips, but since they were sitting amongst her clueless family, she controlled herself from such desires, temporarily.

"Is this Sam someone you know?" Lauren asked in Scarlet's ear, while Juliet smirked at her cousin. "No, but it seems quite suspicious."

The blonde rolled her eyes followed by Juliet, who leaned away from them.

The evening advanced and, the Payne family and the Andersons feasted on the snacks spread out for them while conversing and laughing with each other.

It was a happy evening in the Payne household but wasn't going to stay that way for two certain people that had excused themselves to the kitchen, away from prying eyes and ears.

"What did you want to talk about?" Juliet crossed her arms as she stared at her father, who was stood guiltily in front of her. His eyes said it all, if not his lips that were unmoving and in a thin line.

"I.... I know that you know what I have done."

Juliet straightened before she nodded stiffly at her father, "And?"

Tyler stared at her for a moment, at the resemblance that she had with her mother and himself. "I wanted to say, that I'm...sorry."

Juliet squinted her eyes at him, at her father, who had meant so much to her before she found out what he had done. It wasn't like, he didn't mean anything to her now, she still loved him dearly but the respect she had for him simmered down to nothing. And now here he was standing in front of her, asking for forgiveness when she wasn't even the one he had wronged.

"You should be saying that to mom." She spoke out with a mean tone, and Tyler nodded in agreement. "But, I want you to also know that I'm ashamed of myself, and how sorry I am."

"Okay." It wasn't an okay that meant that everything was back to being fine, neither did it mean that she had forgiven him. It was a word that was said just to let him know that she had listened to his part of the story as well.

It was an acknowledgment.

Chapter 16

The cards were sent, the venue was ready, the dress sat in Vanessa's closet in a cover bag that hid it away from Kevin, the rings were already in Kevin and Vanessa's fingers but then again, they had to place different rings on each other's fingers at their wedding.

So, two new and improved rings were bought as well, that were hidden from both, Vanessa and Kevin's, eyes.

According to Mrs. Anderson, the bride and groom must not look at the rings before their wedding. It was a bad omen.

Vanessa groaned at that and Kevin had caressed her back lovingly with a small smile on his face. He knew how Vanessa was when it came to surprises. She hated them.

Scarlet and Lauren were becoming closer than ever. Lauren forced Scarlet to spend time with her family, when she wanted to stay around Lauren, cuddling in her mattress.

Everything was going good, more than good, great. Everyone was happy and ready for the two love birds to tie the knot already.

Kevin and Vanessa, however were pissed and angry. Who they were angry at: Scarlet, Andrew and Mrs. Anderson.

And how it had come to this; Well, it went something like this:

Scarlet and Blake were sat watching 'The Legend of Kora', with Greg and the twins, when Andrew had entered the living room with a glass of water in his hands, and asked of Vanessa's whereabouts.

Greg, being the only one who knew where they were said this: "They told me that they were going to sleep. Maybe it was because they were awake all night."

Firstly, it was three in the afternoon. Secondly, Scarlet raised an eyebrow and asked Greg with a smile, "How do you know that they were awake?"

"I got up to drink some water, when I heard strange noises coming from their room. It was like they were wrestling in there." Greg giggled innocently while the two adults closest to him, stared at him in horror.

Andrew spitted out most of the water that was in his mouth, before beginning to choke harshly. "Uncle Andrew!" Blake ran up to him and began to beat at his back to stop him from choking. All the while, Scarlet had pulled Greg to her and had started telling him to forget all that he had heard at night.

Greg, who was still too young to understand the ways of adults, only looked at her in confusion with his head tilted adorably.

"Why? What were they doing?" Edward had asked Scarlet, while she rocked Greg back and forth in her lap as to lure him into obeying her.

Andrew, who had survived his choking, began to choke again and this time, Laura rushed into the living room after hearing the harsh gags of her husband.

"Are you okay, honey?" Blake only managed to step aside while holding his laugh, as Laura took his place and began to pat her husband's back.

"Look, let's not talk about this anymore." Scarlet spoke to Greg and the twins that glanced at each other with mischief clear on their faces, that the older woman had failed to notice.

"He just began choking all of a sudden." Blake answered for Andrew, who was starting to turn blue from all the gagging.

"What? Why?" Laura turned to Blake for answers, and he was going to provide them when a certain little boy interrupted. "Why were strange noises coming from Aunty Vanessa and Uncle Kevin's room?"

Scarlet face-palmed as she quickly placed her palm over Greg's mouth, who instantly began to struggle in her hold. "Strange noises?" Laura's face held question as well as her head, as she stared at her daughter for answers, all the while patting her husband on the back.

"Yeah, strange noises like they were wrestling or something." The twins answered their aunt, who halted her movements for a moment, before starting to pat Andrew on the back again but this time, more forcefully.

"They are in so much trouble." Laura's voice was small yet deadly as she turned to Blake, who instantly raised his hands up in fear of what the woman might do. "Call a family meeting this instant."

And Blake had done just that, where The Anderson's were also called, and the result is in front of you.

Kevin and Vanessa were separated – Kevin going to the hotel where his parents were staying – and the kids were brain washed with ice-cream for breakfast.

Lauren had laughed the whole time when Scarlet had told her about everything that went down before Kevin and Vanessa were ordered to stay apart till their wedding.

Kevin and Vanessa had shared some whispers before Kevin was dragged away by the arm by his father, who only waved from over his shoulder at the Payne family, while his mother was smiling all sweetly at Vanessa. "We all have to live without sex for a while, dear." And that's how she parted with them.

"Oh god, my ears! They're bleeding!" Scarlet over-exaggerated as everyone entered the house again, except for the kids, who were still out in the back yard, playing.

"Don't push it, bitch." Vanessa grumbled as she pushed Scarlet by the shoulder and walked away. "Mom, dad! She called me a 'bitch'!"

"Such an insult to dogs." Granny Payne mumbled to herself as she walked away to her room with Pudding yipping here and there in her arms.

Scarlet had heard both of the women and was now sulking while Juliet and Blake tried to console her. Lauren, only smiled at how happy Scarlet was around her family, and wondered how she would part with them once again.

The one thing that Lauren had found out by being close to Scarlet's family for this whole time was the fact that her mother had told everything about Scarlet, to the blonde woman.

At a day when Laura was off to go do the laundry, and Lauren had volunteered to help, just to get closer to the woman that birthed the girl, she was falling in love with.

Lauren had listened to all the little details and the little nostalgic smiles that came to Laura's lips as she talked about her youngest daughter, while separating the white's and the colorful clothes.

"She was like a monkey in her younger days. Always jumping around."

Lauren chuckled as she imagined a little Scarlet, while Laura smiled as she remembered that same little Scarlet.

"And she hated diapers!" Laura's laugh was hearty as she reminisced about all those times that she would chase after the little girl, since she had learned to walk at the age of just 1, and to run after 4 more months.

"But she was always the brightest smiler in the room, in any room that she went in. She stole the hearts of everyone that wanted just a little positivity around them." A smile graced Lauren's lips as she watched Laura fold the clean clothes with a distant look in her eyes.

"She was such a bright kid, but then came her teenage days." It was as if, a fairy tale had been replaced by a sad story. "She changed drastically. I always wondered why she was so distant with us. I still don't know why." Laura sniffed to herself, not wanting the other woman to see her cry over the past.

Lauren could see the sadness taking over Laura's face as she knew in her mind what had brought that distance between them. It was the fact that Scarlet hadn't come out to them, that caused this much space to develop in between their lives and relationships.

"What was she like in high school?" Lauren asked, trying to steer away from the talk of distance and change.

Laura's eyes lit up again as she brought her face up to look at the blonde. "Where do I begin?"

Laura and Lauren chatted about Scarlet the whole evening, as they laughed and smiled together – one speaking of everything that happened in Scarlet's life, as far as she was told, and one imagined everything with the thirst to know Scarlet better.

As these two women talked about a certain dark-haired woman in the basement next to Jared and Wanda's guest room, the same dark-haired girl sneezed continuously in the middle of the living room where Blake and Juliet were also sat.

"Are you sick?" Vanessa had asked as she entered the living room with a coffee cup and a grouchy mood. "No, I think I'm having an allergic reaction to something." Scarlet had answered as she halted her sneezes.

"Maybe, being away from Lauren for just a few hours has made her 'love sick'." Juliet whispered in Blake's ear, who snickered uncontrollably.

"Did you two say something?" Vanessa eyed the two cousins, who shook their heads in unison, with smiles that weren't helping their case much. "Mmhm." Scarlet glared at the two, after a sneeze.

"She's onto us. Run." Blake whispered in Juliet's ear in panic as he immediately got off the couch and sprinted out of the living room.

Juliet face-palmed herself, as Vanessa and Scarlet looked at the entrance of the living room with faces that said only one sentence, 'What the fuck?'

After only a second after his escape, the three women distinctly heard someone fall on the steps of the stairs, and a moment later came a pained voice from outside the living room, "I'm...okay."

Granny Payne was not friendly when she was given less food than usual. She was livid. When Andrew had told Laura to not give her too much of the wonderful smelling and looking pasta, her eyes turned to fire and she was thirsty for blood.

She was only moments away from getting her stick from her room and leaving the house to go hunting for food, more than she was given.

"Why don't we just give her as much as she wants, just for tonight?" Scarlet had reasoned as she nervously smiled. She had noticed her grandmother almost go back to her primal state.

Andrew looked at his youngest daughter's nervous look as she pointed with her eyes towards the old woman that had her old hands clenched tightly into fists.

"May-be you're right." Andrew turned to Laura, who had her hand halted in the pasta bowl. He signaled for her to give her more than a single spoon and she did just that.

Granny Payne, although overjoyed, didn't even glance at Scarlet. Lauren sighed to herself, just like Blake and Juliet, before they all went to eating and conversing again.

At night, Scarlet frowned at Lauren, who had chosen to sleep in her own mattress. "Come on, I said I was sorry." Scarlet whined as she sat up in her head while looking at the laying figure of Lauren, in the darkness of the room.

Blake and Juliet were heavy and quick sleepers, same to the twins. It was only hard to make Greg sleep but other than that, he slept like a baby.

"You stole my ice cream!" Lauren exclaimed in a half- whisper half-scream, while scarlet rolled her eyes. "It was just a spoon."

"A spoon-full."

"Oh, come on, you're over-exaggerating." Lauren's mouth flew open and she turned over in her make-shift bed, showing the dark-haired woman her back. "I'm sorry, Lauren." Scarlet whined as she began to poke the blonde woman with her foot.

"Stop that!" Lauren hissed from over her shoulder as she glared at the other woman. "I'm showw-y." Scarlet pouted adorably, making Lauren's heart start to drum wildly in her chest while her glare melted away.

For a moment, Lauren laid and thought if she should forgive the girl or not. From what, we could tell by so far, was that Lauren loved ice cream and so she came to North Carolina, just so she could be awarded with an ice cream sundae by her brother, for bringing back Scarlet.

She should've known better than steal away even a little bit of her pleasure.

"Okay." Scarlet's face turned into a dazzling smile, one that Lauren hadn't seen before, it was a combination of relief and regret.

"But..." And there came the 'but' to ruin everything. A frown replaced that smile and Lauren felt a little angry at herself for doing that.

"Anything, I'll do anything. I'll buy you an ice cream truck or an ice-cream parlor, you name it." Lauren smiled deviously as she turned around in her mattress.

"Although those two ideas are very tempting, I have something else in mind."

And that's how Scarlet found herself being spooned by Lauren. "I don't like being the small spoon." Scarlet grumbled as she moved in the blonde's arms. "Shut up. Or else I'll go back to my bed."

Scarlet frowned before snuggling back into the blonde's front.

"I can feel your boobs against my back."

Lauren slapped Scarlet's butt, making the other woman jolt forward in surprise. "I can hit your butt."

"Touché."

A normal day in the Payne household.

"Hey, my ass's itchy." Scarlet mumbled sleepily after a long while and Lauren just snuggled closer into the other woman's back, with her arms meeting from around Scarlet's body, at her stomach.

That's how normal days are in the Payne household. Where crazy cousins, hormonal sisters, and wild grandmothers, make your life a living hell. But for Scarlet, this was a hell she wanted to live through once again.

"Why don't you become a lawyer like your sister?" Andrew asked as he stood in the doorway of Scarlet's room.

The – 21-year-old – woman turned to her father and stared in his eyes, in his still loving eyes, as she spoke, "Because I don't want to stay here anymore."

"What's wrong here?" Andrew questioned with a frown as he walked closer to his, busy with packing, daughter.

Scarlet said nothing as she continued to stuff clothes into her suitcase and books into her travelling bag. "Tell me, Scarlet Rose Payne, what is wrong here?" Andrew asked again as he grabbed her arm, halting her packing. He stared into her lying eyes, not even seeing that she had been lying all along, all the time, all the while.

"What is wrong here, please tell me?" His eyes were truthful yet her eyes were betraying herself and him.

But, as her father came close to giving up, she muttered the truth she wanted to suppress. "Because you are here."

"What?" Andrew was taken aback by her answer as he drew his hand away from her wrist. "Because you all are here. Grandma, you, mom, Vanessa." Her voice was firm and her tone bitter and harsh, as her eyes filled up with tears, she didn't let go of.

"I don't want to stay in this small town anymore, that only reminds me of you guys. I hate it so much." Her pain was not transferred into words. Her hate was. Because she hated her grandmother and she hated her sister.

Her grandmother, that only loathed her presence and a sister that had threatened her for having crushes on girls.

Her words still echoed in her mind and she found herself wishing that they didn't, not at a moment where she was facing her father.

"It's just a phase, you'll get over it."

And then she had ripped apart her Selena Gomez poster that hung above her bed.

"Did you really feel that way?" Andrew's broken voice brought back the dark-haired woman back to the present. Without even meaning to, she stared deep into her father's loving eyes and answered, "Yes."

And she began to pack again.

All the while, Laura witnessed on the side what had conspired in the four walls of Scarlet's room. The same exact four walls that held memories and love.

That day, as Andrew walked out of Scarlet's room with only a sad and defeated glance back at the woman that was packing her stuff up, the walls in her room cried. They cried tears of love and memories. The love leaked out from the walls and followed Andrew out of the room.

Not even wondering of where it might go if not back to Scarlet's room.

So, it disappeared in the floorboards, leaving Scarlet's room as bare as the day the house was built. With nothing but painted walls and emptiness.

"She never really did tell us the real reason why she left that day." Laura spoke as she folded up the cleaned-up laundry. "But she did say why she was leaving." Lauren spoke reluctantly as she helped the woman.

Laura shook her head, "She can't fool her mother with a vague answer like that. She had a better and bigger reason for leaving that day."

Lauren glanced at the older woman as she nodded her head, "Maybe she was keeping a secret from you guys."

She couldn't even believe what she had just said to the older woman, who had now halted her hands and had turned to look at Lauren with confusion.

"A secret?" Laura spoke the words as if she wanted to taste them on her tongue and know what they were. "Do you know something?"

Lauren shook her head frantically as she stared into Laura's blue eyes that unfortunately, Scarlet didn't inherit.

"I was just saying."

Laura narrowed her eyes before everything in the laundry room fell silent, with Lauren beating herself up in her head for saying that, and Laura going back in time and remembering if there was something she missed. Even a little detail.

Such as that big poster in Scarlet's room of Selena Gomez, that was one day found teared up in the garbage can. And when she had asked why it was so, Scarlet had answered with this: "She was just a phase." With a bitter underlying tone to her sentence, and a pained and concealed expression on her face.

One thing that Laura was famed for in the Payne family, was for her photographic memory.

And the picture of Scarlet's glazed over eyes, and tight-lipped smile, was very hard to forget.

Chapter 17

"Is Vanessa at the venue already?" Laura asked her husband as she tied her hair in a fashionable bun. Her husband, Andrew, nodded his head while tying his tie. "Yeah, Juliet took her there already."

"And what about Lauren?" Laura asked after she was done with her hair and had moved on to strapping the shoes on her feet.

Juliet and Lauren were Vanessa's bridesmaids and had already left for the venue. Blake and Scarlet had left first in the morning, to go check up on the venue and to pay the old flower lady for her services.

"Oh, that is a bit too much for a little work like this." The old woman spoke as she stared at the large amount of money in Scarlet's hand that was outstretched for the old lady.

"Are you kidding me, this is looking so beautiful!" Blake exclaimed in excitement and Scarlet chuckled before agreeing. "Yes, he has a point, and he rarely has those." Blake snapped out of his excited daze to glare at his cousin while the old woman smiled at the two.

The woman was staring at the two cousins on the verge of having a meaningless argument, when she noticed a flower peeking out of the breast pocket of Scarlet's suit.

"Ah, I think, I've found her secret lover." Both the cousins stopped their mindless quarreling to look at the woman in confusion.

"What?"

The old woman smiled at Scarlet, before she pointed at the flower that was peeking out innocently from her suit's breast pocket. "The Hydrangea symbolizes heart felt emotions."

The dark-haired woman looked down at the flower, before she stared at the woman, still in confusion. "And?"

"Nothing, it's a beautiful flower, isn't it?" Blake and Scarlet glanced at each other before the older cousin nodded her head, still confused of what the old woman wanted to say.

"Well, I think, I'll take my leave now." The woman spoke and Scarlet immediately handed the woman her payment, before she could refuse it again.

The old woman smiled at Scarlet, a smile that meant that she knew something that Scarlet didn't know about.

After the woman, had left, the two walked away from the entrance of the beautifully decorated place and into the small room that was out of the sights of the guests and the groom.

The venue was decorated with the two flowers, roses and forget-me-nots. The aisle had rose petals leading from the entrance of the venue to the altar where the supporting pillars of the small arch like roof was decorated with forget-me-nots.

Since, the wedding was taking place not so far from the Payne house, Vanessa had agreed to change there instead of in the house.

"You look like a princess." Juliet commented with her hands clasped together and her eyes sparkling with excitement, as she looked at her older cousin in awe.

"Thank you, Jules." Vanessa smiled genuinely as she leaned forward to embrace her cousin in a loving hold. "Kevin better keep you like a queen." Vanessa chuckled as she broke the embrace and looked herself in the mirror that was on the wall.

"She's right, Vanessa. You look really beautiful." Lauren spoke as she stood awkwardly beside Juliet. Even though, Vanessa had been mean to her after the time they went to the flower shop, she could not help but to feel a little excited for her wedding.

Lauren still had no idea why Vanessa had picked her to be her bridesmaid alongside Juliet, but she wasn't completely complaining.

A pang of jealousy, though, crept up in her stomach and tried to make her sick.

"Thanks, Lauren." Vanessa looked at Lauren through the mirror and smiled a small but still genuine smile. Lauren reciprocated and nodded.

A knock sounded at the door, and the three women turned their attentions to the door. A minute later, a familiar voice came, "Can we come in, ladies?!"

All three of them rolled their eyes at Blake before Juliet, herself, went to the door and opened it wide, but not wide enough for the boy to see Vanessa. "What?"

Blake glanced at Scarlet, who was smiling at Juliet. "Can we come in?" Juliet narrowed her eyes at her cousins before she gave them a sickeningly sweet smile, "and why do you want to come in?"

"Because the guests are beginning to arrive and we don't know any of them."

"Idiots. Go tend to them, until everyone else are here." Juliet ordered before closing the door back, in their faces. Only groans were heard more, before everything went silent, and Juliet returned to the two women with a satisfied smile on her face.

"Was that Scarlet?" Lauren asked Juliet, who nodded her head, "And Blake." Vanessa watched Lauren with squinted eyes.

"Oh." Lauren looked at Juliet before she turned to the bride, "I'll be right back." Vanessa only managed to nod before the blonde bridesmaid was out of the door and into the fresh air.

Outside, Scarlet and Blake were greeting the guests with large smiles and nods of acknowledgement. Almost everyone that had entered into the venue was either a friend of Kevin or a colleague of Vanessa.

Only when Scarlet had seen her mother and father arrive, did she take a breath of relief. Blake, who was standing beside her in the entrance, also breathed a sigh and bent half with his hands on his knees, as if he hadn't been simply greeting the guests but giving them his air.

"Is Vanessa still getting ready?" Laura had asked as she stood in front of her daughter and nephew. "Yeah, aunty Laura and they were mean to us when we tried to get a look at Van." Blake pouted.

Andrew chuckled before he patted Blake on the shoulder, "I sometimes doubt the fact that you have a brain, my son." Scarlet burst out laughing while Blake pouted some more.

"Where is everyone else?" Scarlet asked as she looked behind her parents. "Well." Andrew began as he looked at his daughter with a guilty smile.

"We kind of left your grandmother to them. So, I think its gonna take them a while."

In the Payne household, everything was in pieces. Not literally, but you get the point.

Granny Payne was angry and her stick was a weapon of defense as she tried to hit anyone with it that came close to her. "I'm not going to be put in a damn wheelchair!" Jared and Tyler glanced at each other as they sighed in annoyance. "Mother, it's going to be a long day. You'll be exhausted even before the wedding starts."

"I don't care!" Granny Payne exclaimed with her hands in the air and her stick following her movements everywhere, while Pudding was holding on to Gregory's leg, who was watching his grandmother from the doorway of her room.

"Come on, Mother! It's only for today!" Tyler tried to get close to her in an attempt to grab her without hurting her. Jared watched his younger brother move and he immediately grabbed the wheelchair from behind him to have it ready whenever Tyler would be successful.

As the two brothers dealt with their old and stubborn mother, Wanda and Judith were sitting in the living room, all ready to go. Edward and Edmund were also sat with their mother and aunt, with their jelled-up hair and tuxedos, and a frown on each of their faces.

"Why?" They both whined in unison and Judith rolled her eyes at her sons. "Because you two would look so cute."

"We don't want to." They crossed their arms exactly at the same time and made their mother and aunt wonder how they could be so in sync with each other.

The two twins were in a bad mood and it was not because of their older cousin's wedding. No. It was because they were going to be used as flower boys at the wedding, which was not taken quite the way Judith had expected.

When Vanessa had come to Judith with the idea of her twin cousins being the flower boys at her wedding, Judith had been excited and had agreed immediately.

But now, she was thinking about a way to get them to do what they were being told to do.

"I'll let you eat ice-cream for breakfast for a week." This caught the twins' attention and they glanced at each other before one of them spoke, "Two weeks."

Judith squinted her eyes, "One and a half."

"Double or nothing, woman." Edward, or maybe Edmund spoke and Judith stared at them for a while before she broke. "Fine, but you are gonna get no allowance for two months."

"Hey! That's practically theft." The twins spoke as they watched their mother smile. "Double or nothing, sweethearts."

Edward and Edmund's mouth flew open and they glanced at each other again before they spat in their right hands and held them out for their mother to shake. "Do I have to spit as well?"

"Yes, or else the deal will be off." Edmund, or maybe it was Edward, spoke with a smirk. They watched their mother spit in her own hand with disgust before shaking her sons' hands one by one.

"Wow, that was some nice bargaining." Wanda muttered to herself as she glanced from the twins to their mother.

In Granny Payne's bedroom, the two brothers were successful in getting their mother in a wheelchair.

"I can't believe what we agreed to do. Andrew is gonna be so mad." Jared spoke as he wheeled his mother out of her room with her stick in the back bag of the wheelchair.

Granny Payne sat satisfied in the rolling chair as she smiled to herself.

Tyler shook his head as he glanced down at his mother. "No telling him anything." Jared nodded with a frown.

Back at the venue, something terrible had just creeped out from the shadows and had taken Lauren with it.

"What are you doing here?" Lauren frowned deeply as she stared at the dyed-blonde haired woman with the blue eyes.

"I was invited." Spoke Katie, "I thought you knew."

Lauren didn't, and that's where the doubts began to resurface from deep inside of her heart.

Chapter 18

"What the fuck are you doing here?" Scarlet was angry, no, scratch that, she was livid, when she saw Stewart coming in from the entrance casually as if it wasn't Scarlet's sister's wedding at all.

"Calm down, Scar. We don't want to make a scene here." Blake held his cousin back, who was trying hard to just punch Stewart once again. "And besides, he's the brother of your girlfriend. You don't want to hear an earful from Lauren." Blake whispered in her ear as he glared subtly at the tall man.

Stewart smirked when Scarlet straightened and just simply glared at him. "To answer your question, I was invited." Scarlet narrowed her eyes while Blake stared at the man with suspicion. "No one invited you." He spoke up as he stood in front of his cousin.

"Oh, I have the card right here." Stewart placed his hand in his suit jacket before pulling out the familiar invitation card that was made precisely for the wedding.

Scarlet stared in shock as Blake snatched away the card and peaked inside.

"Kevin James Anderson and Vanessa Ava Payne invite you Stewart to their wedding." Blake read the card and frowned, "But, I got all the cards delivered."

Scarlet glanced at Blake just as he glanced at her.

Both, of them wondering, who exactly invited the man.

"So, you just tagged along with Stewart?" Lauren crossed her arms as she stared at the girl Scarlet once loved, or still does love, Lauren didn't know for sure.

"Yes, and what a great thing I did coming here. I found out from your brother how much you have gotten closer to her." Katie mirrored Lauren as she herself, crossed her arms as well. "I don't appreciate you getting close to my girlfriend."

"Ex-girlfriend." Lauren pointed out, making Katie glare at her.

"Whatever. We both know that she'll take me back." Lauren knew but she still hoped that Scarlet wouldn't take back Katie as her girlfriend.

"She won't." Lauren spoke with hesitance and that's when Katie took advantage of the blonde woman. "She will, if I just remind her of everything that we did together. We took holidays off together, went on dates, made love, sometimes all night long."

Lauren wanted to rip Katie's head off of her body at the mention of her listing off everything that she had done together with Scarlet and yet had still cheated on her.

"And yet you went out and slept with my brother."

"I wasn't clearly in my senses back then. But, neither was your brother since he didn't mind sleeping with me."

"You're at fault here just as much as Stewart is."

"Are you in love with her?" Katie asked suddenly as she looked at the blonde woman with a questioning look. "Well, it wouldn't even matter if Scarlet isn't in love with you." Katie spoke while dismissing the thought that Scarlet would maybe be in love with Lauren at all.

Lauren deflated when she looked at Katie. Her words now getting to the blonde woman, as she thought inside of her head how she hadn't even been with the older woman for too long for her to fall in love with Lauren.

After a last look at the blonde woman, Katie smiled deviously at Lauren before speaking one last thing to her, "Scarlet only loves me and once I tell her how genuinely sorry I am, she'll definitely take me back."

Lauren didn't say a word as Katie walked away leaving Lauren standing alone at the end of the back of the small room where Vanessa was still sat.

Speaking of Vanessa, the bride was having her body acting up again.

"I have to puke."

"What?" Juliet asked as she stood up from beside the older woman as she clutched her stomach. "I have to puke, Juliet!" Vanessa spoke loudly, making her cousin cuss out colorful words.

"Not in that dress, you won't." Juliet began to unzip her wedding dress as Vanessa tried to control the nauseous feeling.

"Not now, Sam, not now." Vanessa mumbled to herself as she finally got out of the dress and ran to the bathroom.

Juliet rushed into the bathroom as well and held her older cousin's hair as she puked into the toilet bowl.

Laura and Andrew were sitting with Granny Payne as she excitedly talked about how the place looked fantastic. Jared and Tyler were now at entrance duty and often glanced back at their mother.

Wanda was standing beside her youngest son, Gregory, who was holding the rings with a wide smile.

Stewart, who had somehow walked past the dragon – Scarlet – was sitting way at the back, where he tried to call Katie.

"Yeah, where are you?" Stewart spoke into the phone as he looked at the flowers that were almost everywhere. "Here." Came the reply from behind him and he immediately turned back to Katie.

"Well, did you see Scarlet?" Stewart asked as he looked around the place, his eyes searching for the dark-haired ex-employee of his. "No, but I did run into your sister."

Stewart's ears twitched and he looked at her, "You did, where is she?" He wanted to go apologize to her for making things difficult. It was hard to admit but he missed his sister more than anything.

"She was in the back when I last saw her." Katie spoke in an uninterested tone, and Stewart immediately went off to search for her.

The Andersons arrived a while later as they entered the venue with huge smiles on their face.

As Kevin walked down the aisle to take his rightful place, he was stopped by his two friends, one of whom was also the best man at his wedding.

"Jordon, Kyle!" The two men laughed as Kevin embraced them as if he hadn't seen them in years, whereas they had last met him only a couple of months before he came here.

"You look great, how's Hayden and Claire doing?" Kyle laughed while Jordon only nodded his head with an amused smile. "Like they always are. Too much in love."

"Don't be jealous, you two have your times as well with Allison and Natalia." Both the men nodded their heads as they smiled. "Speaking of, where are they?"

"You know how much time the girls take." Kyle waved dismissively as he spoke, "They're probably still at the hotel, I'll call them a while later."

"And Josh and Clayton?"

Kyle and Jordon glanced at each other before they began to look around the place for the two lovers. "They aren't here?"

Kevin frowned when, after searching for a while the two men rolled their eyes, "Probably having sex again, in the back seat of our rental car." Jordon sighed heavily while Kyle smirked.

"They go at it like bunnies." There was amusement in his voice as the two other men laughed.

"Are we too late?" Came a familiar voice from behind the groom and he immediately turned around to embrace the woman in a friendly hug. "Woah, hands off of my girlfriend, stranger." Claire complained as she began to hit Kevin's arm with a playful look in her eyes.

"Oh yeah." Kevin smirked before he picked up the brunette in a hug. "Hayden, make him put me down!" Claire squealed while Kevin laughed at her before placing her back on her feet and getting a slap on the arm.

"Still as aggressive as I remember." Kevin smirked while Claire pouted adorably again.

"Now you know how I deal with the regular abuse." Hayden playfully spoke as she circled her arm around her longtime girlfriend's waist. Claire glared at her girlfriend before pushing her away.

"No more cuddles for you."

"No. I'm sorry, baby." Hayden smiled as she pulled Claire back into her hold and was rewarded with a peck to her lips. "Good girl." Claire smirked at her. The same smirk that had made the other woman fall in love with her.

"See. This is too much love." Kyle complained to Kevin, making the groom laugh in happiness. "What? No love for me." Kevin turned to see the tall figure of his friend as he chuckled and shook his head.

"How could I forget my beard?" Kevin embraced his college friend, Zeke, in a bro hug, getting multiple pats on his back from him.

"I'm happy for you, man." Zeke broke away from the hug and spoke, looking into his friend's eyes. Kevin nodded while the other friends stood with smiles.

Kevin had met Zeke when they were in college, studying for business. That was when Zeke had introduced Kevin to his other friends and from then on, they all became a close knit group.

Jordon and Kevin began to work together at their garage where they mostly repaired cars but here and there did some unique metal work as well.

"Did Josh and Clayton not get here?" Zeke asked quizzically as he looked around at the place that was now considerately filled with people.

Jordon and Kyle rolled their eyes, while Hayden and Claire only glanced at each other before one of them shrugged and the other smirked, immediately knowing why they weren't with them.

"I'll bet you 20 dollars saying that they're probably fucking in our rental car." Claire smirked with her eyes shining with amusement. Hayden glanced at her girlfriend before shaking her head, "They're grown men now, I don't think they'll be that irresponsible to repeat their past mistakes."

Jordon and Kyle were shaking their heads at Hayden, signaling her to not bet with Claire but she did anyway, "30, saying that they're probably stuck in traffic." Claire smirked making Hayden's heart beat in her chest as she smiled.

A minute later, Josh and Clayton walked casually down the aisle but stopped when they saw the groom and the rest of their friends.

"Kevvy!" Josh exclaimed before he ran up to the groom and hugged him tightly.

Clayton had his hair ruffled up, and by the way his hair was shining, was reason enough to know that he had gelled up his hair but something happened and now his hair was sticking up from everywhere.

Claire only held out her palm for her girlfriend, who grumbled about how indecent her friends were as she took out a crisp 30-dollar bill out from her pants pocket.

"We warned you." Kyle patted Hayden's back as she glared at the two 'newly' arrived friends of hers.

Kevin smiled widely as he hugged Josh dearly before opening up his arms for Clayton, who rolled his eyes, "You do know that I don't hug." Josh stared at Clayton with a 'what the fuck' look, before the man sighed and embraced Kevin in a bro hug.

"I'm just doing this because Josh said so." Kevin laughed heartily before breaking their hug and watching his friends all rejoiced except for Allison and Natalia.

"I'll introduce you guys to Vanessa's sister after I find her, okay?" Kevin smiled as he spoke with his voice showing how happy he truly was now.

"Have you even told Aunt Laura or even Uncle Andrew?" Juliet asked as she sighed loudly. "No, no one knows, only Kevin and I do."

"We have to tell them before the wedding." Juliet spoke as she began to straighten out her dress. Vanessa looked at her cousin with horror as she grabbed her wrist, halting her next movements.

"We can't." Juliet frowned as she stared at the bride. "What do you mean, we can't?"

"I mean, we can't tell them or else they'll be angry at me." Vanessa spoke as a bit insecurity seeped through her tone. "I don't want them to be angry at me or even at Kevin. I know, dad would try to murder him right there and then."

Juliet nodded before she sighed heavily, plopping down on a nearby sofa. "So, what do we do?"

A knock interrupted the thoughts of the two women as they glanced at each other with eyes filled with terror as if someone had already found out about their secret.

Juliet stood up and walked to the door with quick yet careful steps.

Opening the door, she came face-to-face with a smiling Blake and Scarlet, "The priest is here."

Juliet could only glance back at Vanessa before gulping down the secret she had just heard and smiling back at her two cousins.

"She'll be right out." The two frowned as they could see the clear discomfort in her face but before they could call her out on it, she shut the door in their faces.

"The priest is here."

Chapter 19

With nothing but self-pitying thoughts in her head, Lauren sat in the grass, not even caring about her dress.

All the things that Katie had said were eating away at her and she was only wondering how she could just disappear without anyone knowing.

Her thoughts were interrupted when she heard the familiar voice of her brother call out to her.

"There you are!" Stewart spoke with a smile but it was soon turned into a frown when he saw the tears that were pooled inside of the blonde woman's eyes and the quivering of her lips.

"What happened?" Stewart asked with worry lacing his each and every word. Lauren smiled a little before she uttered the three words she had never before, speaking them and tasting them on the tip of her tongue as she let them go from her heart to her mouth and then out into the world.

It was no secret anymore, but a bittersweet feeling.

"I love Scarlet."

The priest was standing at the altar, "Everyone, please stand." He announced as he looked around at the people that were occupying the seats.

Kevin stood smiling at the altar with his two best men – Kyle and Zeke – beside him. Gregory was standing near the altar with Wanda and the two wedding rings.

Everyone's eyes went to the entrance where Edward and Edmund came out from with baskets full of rose petals, as they took fistfuls and lined the path with the petals.

Judith smiled to herself when she saw her sons.

Only a minute later, music began to play and Vanessa walked into the sights of everyone with Juliet guiding her.

Both of their faces were filled with worry as they glanced at each other before walking two more steps, where Andrew stood with a smile and his left arm outstretched for his daughter to take.

"Tell him now." Juliet whispered in Vanessa's ear before she went away to sit beside her father, in the second row.

Vanessa's eyes followed her red-headed cousin before she turned to her father and gave him a smile, linking his arm with her own.

Andrew's smile didn't waver as he began to walk his daughter down the aisle. "I'm so proud of you, Vanessa. I've always been proud of you." Andrew began to speak while Vanessa tried to gulp down the rising bile in her throat.

"I'm so happy to see you this happy with Kevin. He'll make you even happier, than I ever did."

"No, dad. You'll always be the first man in my life, you made me happier than anything. Believing in me and taking care of me." Vanessa spoke with her eyes tearing up.

Her father chuckled before he swiped at his eyes. "Don't go making your old man cry with praise, now."

Vanessa giggled through her throat that was beginning to close up.

"Um, dad?"

Andrew nodded in acknowledgement as he eyed Kevin, who was smiling widely at the two.

"I need to tell you something."

"I'm listening."

"It's...uh, I......I'm pregnant, daddy." Andrew halted his steps and Vanessa closed her eyes tightly to not see what his father's reaction would be.

They were only a few steps away from the altar and everyone had noticed how they had stopped abruptly. Whispers began almost immediately and Kevin stared at his bride with a confused expression on his face.

"That bastard." Andrew's face contorted into one of anger and he balled his fists up with only one objective in mind as he saw Kevin's face. To feel his knuckles hit Kevin's jaw as hard as they could.

"No, daddy. It's not his fault." Mr. Andrew Payne was livid as he saw red. "I was the one that....." She couldn't continue her sentence because of a certain man.

"You, heartless bitch!" Stewart exclaimed as he tackled a, standing in the back with Blake, confused Scarlet. The dark-haired girl fell to the ground with the man over her as he sniffed like a little girl.

"I hurt you that doesn't mean that you have to hurt my little sister!" Scarlet stared at the man in confusion and anger as she tried to push him off of her.

Everyone in their seats were now fully turned around as they watched Scarlet and Stewart on the carpet having a fight.

Andrew was still seeing red and after seeing Scarlet's ex-boyfriend tackling her to the ground, he saw blood red and he stalked over to the two with his fists clenched while Juliet came over to Vanessa's side and began to ask questions.

"Did you tell him?" She asked in a whisper as she watched Blake and Andrew try to pry Stewart off of Scarlet.

"Yes." Vanessa spoke with tears already pooling in her eyes. "He'll kill Kevin." Juliet caressed Vanessa's back as she tried to calm her down.

"Get off of her, you idiot!" Blake spat before he was successful in prying the man off of his cousin.

"I knew you were trouble when I first saw you!" Andrew piped in as he grabbed Stewart by his collar and leaned in close to his face. "You better leave son, before, you might not be able to do so."

Scarlet, who had stood up again and was now dusting herself off, was as angry as her father as she saw the one face she didn't want to see again.

"What are you doing here?" Her voice didn't come out as angry as she had thought it would, it came out broken and pitiful.

Katie smiled a small smile before she walked closer to her ex-girlfriend and planted her lips firmly on to her lips.

The whole place erupted in gasps as Katie moved her lips against unmoving ones, trying desperately to convey her true feelings through a kiss, since she couldn't convey them through words anymore.

Scarlet's eyes squeezed shut as she felt Katie's lips trying to move against hers, and only one thought moved inside her mind.

How Katie's lips were nothing like Lauren's.

Pushing the woman off of her, Scarlet harshly wiped her lips as she took in the features of the girl she used to love. "What are you doing?" Katie stared at the older woman with worry etched in her face.

"I........I'm sorry for cheating on you."

"What?!" Before Scarlet could even understand what had happened, she saw her mother stand up from her seat in the first row and stare at Scarlet with a betrayed look.

"Mom, I can explain!"

Scarlet's secret was out.

"Oh gosh." Juliet mumbled before palming her face. Vanessa, who had controlled her tears had already forgotten about how she had told her father about the little life that was now inside of her.

"You.....you cheater!" Stewart pointed accusingly at Scarlet, as he tried to wiggle free from Blake's hold. "What are you even talking about?!" Scarlet stared at Stewart with her eyebrows knotted together in anger, completely trying to ignore the woman standing in front of her.

"You better not be ignoring me, young lady!" Laura exclaimed from behind Scarlet while Stewart yelled from in front of her. "You got my sister, my innocent, sweet sister to fall for you and then you go ahead and dare choose Katie over her! Over her!" Scarlet's eyes widened in realization as she looked at him.

"What? I didn't even....... Why would you even say that?" At this Scarlet began to look around the people in search of the blonde woman that she had begun to fall for. When she couldn't find her, her eyes automatically turned to Katie, who was now clearly uncomfortable in the whole environment.

She never did like being put at the spot.

"What did you say to her?" Katie couldn't even face Scarlet as she sniffed.

Before, when Katie was ashamed of something or guilty for doing something wrong, she would immediately begin to cry, and Scarlet being the love-sick person she was, would always forgive her. But at the moment, when Katie began to tear up, Scarlet's eyes blazed and she immediately pushed passed the woman to stalk over to Stewart, who was now just watching his ex-employee.

"Where is she?" Scarlet asked and Stewart tried to cower in Blake's hold – who was also shaking from the venomous voice of his cousin – but Scarlet made sure that he didn't. "I don't know...... she should be here."

She wasn't.

"Did she tell you where she went?" Scarlet persisted as she tried to ignore the scared feeling that was trying to creep up into her stomach. "No."

"Scarlet, I'm really sorry for cheating on you, but please don't choose her." Katie's voice was broken and shaky as she grasped the dark-haired woman's arm.

Scarlet sighed, trying to push away her anger from taking over her. "I'm the one that should be sorry, Katie."

Everyone watched as Scarlet turned back around to face Katie, who had her tears now freely trailing down her cheeks.

For some, it looked like a lover's quarrel, for others it was like a live show that they could possibly never be able to see again.

But for the Payne family, it was the truth.

"I can't believe, we were raising an abomination under our roof." Granny Payne, who was sitting in the first row spoke as she stared at Scarlet.

"Mother!" Tyler exclaimed as he looked at the old woman in disbelief. "What? What did I say wrong?"

"You didn't say anything wrong, mother." Jared backed her up as he stared at his younger brother with his eyes speaking what his mouth wasn't.

"No," Tyler paused to glance at his daughter before continuing again, "you both are wrong."

Judith teared up as she stood up from her seat, "Your thinking is wrong." Granny Payne stared at her youngest son and daughter-in-law, in surprise as Tyler began to tear up as well, before he spoke about what was really wrong.

The fact that he had cheated on his wife with a man and she had forgiven him. That was wrong and yet right.

Because there is nothing completely wrong in life without being a little bit right.

"I don't want to be with you anymore." Scarlet spoke as she looked at her ex-girlfriend.

Katie's tears still flowed as she stared into the dark-haired woman's eyes, the eyes that she found love in. There was love in Scarlet's eyes but the love wasn't for Katie anymore.

"Is it because you don't love me anymore?" Katie asked sniffing. Scarlet's eyes closed for a second, seeing only the face of the blonde woman, before opening them back up again.

"It's not that I don't love you, because I do." Scarlet grabbed Katie's hand in her own, trying to keep her own tears from pooling inside of her eyes.

It wasn't so easy to let someone go, but it also wasn't easy to let someone go when that someone only has you in their heart.

"You liar, mm....!" Stewart was cut off when Blake's hand came up to place itself on to his mouth.

"I still love you, Katie." Katie sighed when Scarlet raised her hands and caressed her cheeks that still had tears staining them, "But I'm in love with Lauren."

Stewart's eyes widened as well as everyone's around them.

Laura stepped back a little while Vanessa frowned, "I knew there was something going on between them."

"Before you say anything about phases, let me repeat what Scar just said. She said that she's in love with Lauren." Juliet glared at Vanessa, who only stared at her younger cousin in disbelief.

Vanessa had opened her mouth to speak when Juliet raised her hand, halting her words, "And yes, I did know about their relationship." That was all Vanessa needed to know for her to shut up completely.

"I don't understand!" Katie cried as she closed her eyes, making Scarlet breath out a shaky sigh, "I don't understand either, but I don't think that I can go back with you to New York and resume the life I had without being unhappy, without making you unhappy."

Katie cried some more as she wrapped her arms around Scarlet's neck and pulled herself into the warmth of the dark-haired woman. "Please, I'm sorry." Katie hiccupped as she nuzzled into the older woman's shoulder trying to make them one somehow, then maybe, just maybe, Scarlet wouldn't leave her.

"I'm sorry." Scarlet spoke before she was backing away from Katie's hold. "I can't be with you anymore."

And before anyone would stop her, she turned around and ran out of the place with only the shouts of her family following her.

Kevin, who had only been standing at the altar, came towards his bride, "Are you okay?" Juliet had gone over to Blake, whose face was now drenched in tears as he still held Stewart in a tight hold.

"Stop crying, you buffoon, we have to follow her." Juliet slapped him on the arm, and then glared at Stewart, who was mumbling incoherent words against Blake's palm.

"What is he saying?" Juliet asked quizzically while Blake controlled his tears. "I don't know." Blake answered with his face contorted into a frown. "If you take off your hand, we might know." Juliet sarcastically spoke as she grabbed Blake's arm and began to drag him towards the entrance, who in turn dragged Stewart with them.

Blake's mouth formed an 'o' and he immediately took away his hand from the man's mouth but not away from his arm. "I said." Stewart spoke glaring at Blake, "we can follow her in my car."

"We? There's no we. There's only Blake and I, which makes it 'us', not we."

Stewart rolled his eyes at the redhead before he took out his car keys from his pants pocket. "It's a 'we' since I have the keys."

Juliet sighed before she nodded at the man, making him smirk.

The three had made their way to the parking lot and Stewart lead them towards his car, more like towards the place where he parked his car.

"Where's my car?!" Stewart looked around frantically as if the thief would still be at the crime scene.

"Uh, I think Scar took it." Blake spoke as he picked a piece of tissue paper, which had only a sentence written on it.

Juliet came closer to Blake and inspected the delicate paper before she burst out in laughter, "what? What's written on it?"

Stewart looked from over Blake's shoulder and immediately groaned loudly.

The tissue paper said: Sorry for breaking a window.

The wedding was stopped and the guests were still entertained.

After Scarlet, had left the area, and the three followed her, all hell broke loose.

Vanessa confronted the still crying girl, and trust me, she had a lot to say to the crying blonde.

"It all makes sense now. You cheated on her with that man." Vanessa spoke as she was now stood in front of Katie, who was sat in the last row with her head down and her eyes still crying a river.

Laura had gone over to the blonde to try to comfort her, even when she wanted nothing more than to ask her if Scarlet had ever talked about her family to her, because she hadn't talked about Katie to them at all.

"Was Scarlet such a lousy lover that you had no other choice but to cheat on her with a man?" Vanessa laughed maniacally while Kevin tried to pull her away from the crying blonde. "I'm sorry." Katie had just mumbled while crying.

"I hope that the little bit of love that Scarlet has left for you, goes away as well." She spat angrily before she allowed herself to be pulled away from the blonde by her groom.

Only a second later, Vanessa was now in tears as she hid away her face from everyone else and cried out into her groom's shoulder, ruining her own makeup and soaking up her husband-to-be's tuxedo.

"Ssh, it's okay." Kevin soothed her back, while she cried. "Sam wouldn't like his mother being such a cry-baby." He tried to joke, in hopes that his bride would feel better, and smiled when Vanessa chuckled brokenly.

"I was such a horrible sister to Scarlet." Vanessa spoke into Kevin's clothed shoulder as she remembered all the times she had bullied her into believing that what she was feeling was just a phase.

Now, she was regretting everything, and more than anything, she was regretting ever being cruel to Lauren, and hurting her with words that always took more time to heal than wounds or scars.

Andrew stood beside his mother, who had a permanent frown on her face as she stared at the ground. She wondered if all the times she had tortured Scarlet was worth the hurt she felt as well.

Jared and Tyler were sitting beside each other but too far away to even notice the distance they had now between them.

"Do you boys remember your father?" Granny Payne asked as her eyes looked distant and detached, while her voice was far away as well.

Andrew, Jared and Tyler snapped out of their own thoughts to acknowledge their mother's.

"Yes, mama. Why are you asking about him so suddenly?" Jared asked as he glanced at his two brothers questioningly.

"He told me something just before his last breath." Granny Payne spoke as a small smile came over her face. The three brothers listened intently as they looked at their mother.

"He told me that he loved me and how every day with me and with you three was the best of his life." She continued, glancing at every one of her sons. "Dad was a great man." Andrew chimed in as he nodded his head at the old woman. "But I don't understand why you're telling us all of this, so suddenly?"

Granny Payne shook her head as her eyes darkened a little. "He wasn't completely truthful with us, my children."

"What are you saying, mama?" Jared asked and the old woman sighed heavily as if there was a heavy load on her heart. "Before he died, he told me that he was never happy."

Before her sons would speak that it wouldn't be so, Granny Payne continued with her voice cracking at some points, "We were best of friends, and he had never told me of how he was attracted to other men. He had asked me to marry him and I had said yes, thinking that maybe he loved me too, as much as I loved him, and he did. But that love was never like the love I had for him."

Tyler fidgeted in his seat as he stared at his mother, who was now on the verge of breaking down into tears. "He told me, on his death bed, how he didn't regret ever marrying me or having such wonderful children with me. But that he regretted never telling me that he had fallen in love with a man, and being afraid of people, he had suppressed his feelings. He regretted lying to me."

Andrew placed his arm around his mother as a means of support and comfort. "He told me that he loved me, and yet he never was in love with me."

Andrew nodded, just as the two others did as well, "I'm sorry for treating Scarlet so cruelly." Granny Payne had now turned herself completely towards Andrew, as she apologized. "She just reminded me so much of Harold."

"I understand, mother." Andrew nodded again and she sighed loudly. "I wish, she would too, and forgive her old grandma."

"I can't forget her and move on. She's my everything." Katie cried into her hands as she spoke in muffled words, to the mother of her officially ex-lover.

"Sometimes it's painful to move on, but it doesn't mean that its unnecessary." Laura patted the crying woman's back as she looked at the annoyed priest sitting on the steps of the altar.

Most of the guests were gone, but some remained.

Kevin's friends were still there as well as the Andersons, who clearly had no idea of what was going around them.

"I can't live without her." Katie spoke in tears as she raised her head from her hands to look at the older woman. "I didn't mean to cheat on her, it just happened."

"And she knows that too, I'm sure of it, but you have to understand, Lauren was there when she needed someone the most." Laura spoke as she beated herself up for not seeing something so clear and obvious.

The clothes, the wanting to leave their home, the detachment from family time, everything was in front of her and waiting to be noticed. "You're not at fault here, and neither is she, but if she had gone back to you, are you completely sure, she would've been the same person you fell in love with?"

Katie stared at the woman as her mind circled around before coming to a rather sad answer. "No."

Laura nodded her head and wrapped an arm around the blonde's shoulder, providing with her, comfort and understanding.

Vanessa was sat next to Kevin, with her head on his shoulder while he whispered sweet nothings into her ear, when Andrew approached them.

Being the first one to notice the man coming towards them, Vanessa immediately stood and was followed by Kevin, who took his time standing up with confusion clear on his face at her bride's sudden reaction.

"Dad, I can explain."

"I don't need an explanation." Andrew spoke with a defeated sigh as he plopped down on the seat beside Vanessa's. The bride stared at her father in question before she sat back down.

Kevin, who had an idea of why he was there, slipped away from them without letting them notice that he had left them alone.

"Did you know that Scarlet liked girls?" Andrew asked as he stared at the decorated altar which was somewhat mocking him.

The bride and groom, both, were there and yet the wedding was not continuing on from where it had been left off.

Vanessa's eyes casted downwards as she nodded her head ashamed of the thought of not even understanding her own sister.

"I always thought it was a phase."

Andrew snorted with his arms crossed in front of his chest as he swiped at his left eye. "So, she really did want to marry Selena Gomez?" Vanessa smiled remembering Scarlet's passionate talk of how she was going to grow up and marry the beautiful singer.

"Yeah. She was mad for her."

Andrew glanced at his oldest daughter before addressing the elephant that was floating around in the open space, trying to be noticed.

"Is it a boy or a girl?" Vanessa looked at her father before her eyes teared up a little and her hand unconsciously went to her small and unnoticeable baby bump.

"We don't know, since it's too early, but we decided to name it Sam." Andrew nodded and Vanessa waited for him to scream at her for being careless and getting pregnant before marriage or how it was against their family rules, but nothing came, and she just waited.

The silence was speaking for itself as Andrew placed an arm around his oldest daughter's shoulders and Vanessa leaned herself into him and cried on his chest, while he tried to stop her from doing so.

"At least you don't have to care about Scarlet ever getting pregnant." Vanessa mumbled in her father's chest and the man laughed a heartily. Vanessa finding comfort in the way he laughed.

No one could ever replace the sound of his laughter. Certainly, some could rival it, but never actually replace.

And Vanessa knew why.

Because it was calming and protecting, like a shield made from arms, or like a candle lighting up the dark. Or simply, a warm blanket in a cold winter.

His laughter spoke for itself, that, "It's okay."

"Man, thanks for inviting us here. That was the best preshow I've ever seen." Clayton laughed before he was hit on the head by his boyfriend. "Behave, Clay."

"But seriously, are they gonna be alright?" Claire asked as she glanced at the back row at the blonde that had now stopped crying. "It looked pretty intense to me."

Kevin nodded before smiling, "They'll be alright."

Chapter 20

"Lauren!" Scarlet entered the house and was welcomed by silence and the mixture of perfumes that her family used. Other than that, there was nothing.

She quickly rushed up the stairs and went towards the rooftop first. Maybe she was there.

When she reached the rooftop, there wasn't any sign of the blonde woman. Deflated, Scarlet went back down and sighed loudly, before her mind told her to check the guest room.

She slapped herself in the face for being an idiot, and for not checking the guest room first, because when she had reached the guest room, she found a packed suitcase, but still not a blonde woman.

Scarlet walked inside of the room with a frown when she saw that the only evidence of Lauren staying in the room was her red suitcase, which looked completely packed.

A second later, when the bathroom door opened, Scarlet saw Lauren, and for certain reasons, it felt like she was seeing her for the very first time. As if, they had time travelled back to that photo shoot where Scarlet was standing impatiently, tapping at her notebook, waiting for the damn photographer to relieve the model from her posing duties.

Lauren looked just as perfect as she did, when she was in that god-awful dress, that looked extra-large on her but she seemed to be rocking it nonetheless.

"Hi." It came out more awkward than it sounded in Scarlet's brain as she took a step towards the blonde woman, only a small step.

Lauren's heart beated wildly as she stared at Scarlet, with questions that her mind answered for her.

Maybe she came here to tell me face to face, how she chose Katie over me. She thought to herself as she tried to smile at the dark-haired woman.

"Hey." Her voice sounded tired and defeated as she turned away from Scarlet and went over to her suitcase.

Scarlet noticed the way Lauren was dressed, in a dress that hugged her body like second skin, and was showing skin which in Scarlet's mind felt like too much.

Scarlet cleared her throat before she began, "I came here to tell you that I-"

"I know what you're going to say." Lauren spoke up without looking back at the woman that had begun to mean everything to her. "You do?" Scarlet asked with a nervous laugh as she scratched the back of her head awkwardly.

"Yeah." Lauren tried to sound brave but in the end failed miserably as her voice cracked. "I hope she doesn't hurt you again."

Scarlet's smile faded as she stared at Lauren's backside with confusion, "What?"

Lauren sighed before she turned around and stared straight into the older woman's eyes with her own green pools that looked like the trees had melted just to compete with the ocean, which was only one of a kind and impossible to beat.

Scarlet was about to say something when her phone started ringing. She sighed heavily before raising a finger towards Lauren as to tell her to wait a minute.

Placing the phone by her ear, she spoke, "What?"

"Scarlet Rose Payne, is that a respectable way to talk to your mother?" Scarlet brought the phone away from her ear to look at the caller id and sighing loudly, "No mother."

"Good."

"Aunt Laura, that isn't why we called her." Came the familiar voice of Edward, or was it Edmund.

"Scarlet, I swear to you, if you don't return my car in the way it was before, I won't let you date my sister!" Stewart yelled from the other side of the phone, making Scarlet groan in annoyance.

"Hush up, Stew." Juliet's voice spoke before Scarlet heard muffled noises, "There we go." Blake's voice floated into Scarlet's ear.

Lauren had her eyes trained on Scarlet, as she watched the dark-haired woman for the last time.

She had planned to use Stewart's private jet and fly back to New York without telling the woman, but since Scarlet was here, she decided to at least say goodbye.

"Where are you?" Came Juliet's voice again as she asked the dark-haired woman. Scarlet rolled her eyes before answering, "At home."

"Good. Is Lauren there with you?" She questioned and Scarlet glanced at Lauren before speaking, "Yeah."

"Wonderful."

"Put us on speaker!"

"Damn it, Edmund! Why don't you just shut up?!"

"He's not Edmund, I am!"

"Sorry."

"I'm just kidding, I am Edmund." A pause, before, "Ow, mom!"

Scarlet rolled her eyes before she practically screamed, "Guys!", making Lauren flinch at the loudness.

"Sorry." Scarlet apologized as she looked at Lauren with a little coloring on her cheeks.

"Put us on speaker!" Greg's loud voice came through and Scarlet obeyed her little cousin.

Putting her family on speaker, Scarlet only gave Lauren an awkward smile before she brought her phone from her ear to her front, so that they could hear her as well as she could too.

"Now, have you told Lauren that you love her!?" Blake's voice drifted from the phone to Lauren's ears that twitched and stood in attention.

"What?" Lauren's voice was loud enough for the Payne family to hear through the phone and instantly a string of complaints and whacking noises were heard.

"Lauren! Forget that I ever said that!"

"You nincompoop!"

"Grandma! Hit him on the head with your stick!"

As the voices mashed together in the silence of the two women, Lauren stared at Scarlet with confusion and a little happiness that tried to surface and expand, even when she wasn't sure that what Blake had said was true or not.

Scarlet felt herself shying away as Lauren's intense gaze burned into her. She wanted to tell her that she loved her but her words were stuck in her throat.

And then she remembered a flower that a certain blonde had given her, meaning heartfelt emotions.

Taking the peeking flower out of her jacket's breast pocket, Scarlet took the remaining five more steps and closed the distance between them.

Lauren watched with her emotions getting the better of her, and her smile trying not to spread out on her face too much, as Scarlet shyly held out the flower to her.

"It symbolizes heartfelt emotions. And my heart feels love for you." Lauren's vision blurred as she practically threw herself into Scarlet's arms and burst out into tears on her shoulder.

"My heart feels the same way." Scarlet's heart rate accelerated unhealthily fast as she wrapped her arm around the blonde's body, trying to get rid of even the little space between them.

"Aww!"

"Way to ruin the mood, shithead!"

"Language, young lady!" Scarlet and Lauren giggled as Juliet was getting scolded.

"Sorry, grandma!"

"Wait, grandma?" Scarlet's eyes widened as well as Lauren's as they broke away their hug and looked at the phone in Scarlet's hand as if it was going to show them the answers to their unanswered questions.

"If you both are done being selfish! Get your butts back here, so that Kevin and I can get married!"

"Vanessa?"

"Yeah, I won't even try to make you watch straight porn!" Jared's voice came through the phone and Scarlet laughed, as she remembered the little talk Blake and her had in the park close to their house.

"What's porn, mommy?"

"Jared!"

"Oops. I meant corn, son."

Scarlet laughed as she heard the mixed voices of her family which wasn't even in the slightest bit bothered by her sexuality.

"Let me speak, you boogers!" A loud voice came through the phone and the two lovers could hear that everyone else had quieted down.

"Scarlet."

"Yes?" Scarlet spoke reluctantly as she heard her grandmother's voice which was loud enough and clear.

"I'm sorry for being such a bad grandmother to you."

"No, grandma. You-"

"Let me speak, child."

Scarlet silenced herself as her grandmother continued, "You were always such a kind kid, and I was always so hateful towards you….. The day that you were born, I was so happy that you resembled your grandfather so much. Every little feature of yours was just like your grandfather's. But when he died……"

There was a pause as Scarlet heard the little sobs of her grandmother, "When he died, just a day after your birth, I was filled with anger and hate, useless anger and hate, and I took it all out on you."

Scarlet sniffed herself, and the blonde grasped her hand in her own, giving the dark-haired woman a sweet and supportive smile.

"I never hated you, Scarlet."

"I know you didn't, grandma." Scarlet spoke back as she smiled.

"People! I have a life growing inside of me that is hella hungry and my ring finger feels empty! Can we please talk about my wedding now?!"

"Yeah, yeah, yeah, it's all about Vanessa!"

"Put a sock in it, Allison!"

"Hey, Kevin, control the bridezilla!"

"Who you calling a bridezilla!?"

"They won't mind if we hang up on them, right?" Scarlet asked with a mischievous smile as she looked at her blonde lover. "Scarlet Rose Payne! Don't you dare hang up on us!"

Lauren giggled when Scarlet groaned loudly.

"Damn it."

"Mommy, what does 'damn it' mean?"

"Scarlet!"

Scarlet laughed as Aunt Wanda yelled at her for saying bad words in front of Gregory, well technically not in front of him, but you get the drift, right?

"Shall we, pretty lady?" Scarlet held out her free hand for Lauren to take, who giggled before taking it.

"Scarlet sucks at being romantic." Juliet laughed as well as someone else that sounded oddly like Blake. "I don't suck at beating someone's ass, so you two better be standing when I get there." Scarlet spoke into the phone, getting another giggle from her blonde lover while they descended the stairs.

"Ass!"

"Gregory, you shouldn't be saying that word!"

Blocking out the phone conversation, happening in the phone, Scarlet glanced at Lauren, who had a happy smile on her face, as they got out of the house, locking it before heading to Stewart's car which had a broken window.

"Is that Stewart's car? You broke his window?" Lauren laughed as Scarlet smiled sheepishly.

"I'll kill you Scarlet! Lauren, if you're there, don't let her get into my car again, I forbid you from dating a violent woman like her!"

Lauren's laugh was sweet as she stared at Stewart's car, before turning to Scarlet. "I don't know why but I've fallen a few more feet in love with you just from seeing this."

Scarlet grinned before she opened the passenger side door for Lauren and then going over to the driver's side.

When both of them were in the car, and the phone was still in call, Lauren turned to Scarlet after noticing the dress she was now wearing, "I need to change back into the bridesmaid's dress."

Scarlet glanced down at her clothes before she waved her off dismissively, "You don't need to. Vanessa would understand."

"I hate you for choosing this day for being honest. You could've just come out before or after my wedding." Vanessa kept hitting Scarlet on her shoulders as she ranted intensely.

"Because of you, most of the guests left. The priest, was even about to leave but Kevin had to pay him extra for staying overtime."

The Payne family laughed as Vanessa kept up her assault on her little sister. "I'm having cramps now because of hitting you." She complained as she breathed deeply before glaring at Scarlet, who took all of her hits with a smile on her face.

"You look really beautiful, Van-hell. Did I tell you that?"

Vanessa's lower lip twitched before she threw her arm around her sister's shoulder, "I'm crying again, because of you."

"I know, I know."

Lauren smiled as she stood next to Stewart, who had now somehow controlled his anger after seeing his car whimpering in pain due to the broken door window.

"Her family's crazy." He commented as he stared at the mass of the Payne family members, now group hugging. "But they're good folks."

"I know."

"Scarlet…. She'll keep you happy." Stewart glanced at his sister, who was already looking at him with a loving smile. "I know."

"Would it be weird if I say that her red headed cousin is cute?" Lauren's face contorted in disgust before she laughed, "I don't think you have a chance with her."

"I know." Stewart chuckled as the two of them bumped shoulders with each other.

Epilogue

"I request everyone to please rise." The priest spoke to the few handful of people that remained on the seats.

The Payne family, Kevin and Vanessa's friends, and the Andersons.

Edward and Edmund skipped up the aisle, showering it with rose petals and laughs as their baskets full of petals dangled in their arms.

After the two had completed their journey to the altar, they went towards the two seats where their mother was. Juliet and Lauren entered through the entrance, with Vanessa behind them. Each had a bouquet of roses in their hands, grasping them as if to show the groom, standing at the altar a promise of love, from the bride.

Vanessa walked behind them, with Andrew accompanying her, with tears in his eyes and a smile playing on his lips. In Vanessa's hands, were the beautiful forget-me-nots that were a promise by itself, of eternal love.

The morning sky had turned into the pre-evening scene as the sky was painted in red and yellow mixed with blue.

No words were exchanged when Andrew placed Vanessa's hand in Kevin's, only a few actions were done.

A few shoulder pats here and there, showing the trust Andrew had begun to have for the man, and a few smiles that were larger than life itself, showing the love that was there whenever they needed it.

"You all can now be seated."

Scarlet smiled and winked at the blonde woman, who was standing at the side of the bride with Juliet. Lauren giggled behind her hand before she blushed a red color.

Stewart tried to wink playfully at Juliet, who responded with her hand clutched into a fist, and he immediately looked away.

Kyle and Zeke stood at the side of the groom, staring at their group of friends that weren't being loud with words or cheers, but by their actions.

Josh was practically weeping into Clayton's shoulder, while the bad boy tried to nicely shut him up.

Claire was resting her head on Hayden's shoulder, with her arm practically entangled with the black-headed woman's. Allison was handing Josh some tissue papers from her purse.

While Jordon was showing his thumbs up to Kevin, who appreciated the gesture.

"Dearly beloved," The priest began to speak, "we are gathered here this evening to witness this man and woman join together in holy matrimony."

He said the speech, during which Kevin and Vanessa stared lovingly into each other's eyes before they began to speak their vows.

"I, Kevin James Anderson, take you, Van-hell, to be my lawfully wedded wife, friend and lover till death do us apart."

"Yeah, Van-hell!"

Vanessa rolled her eyes playfully.

Kevin smiled at her apologetically before continuing, "In the presence of our family and friends, I give my solemn word to cherish you as my half and take care of you in sickness and in health, to be there with you in the bad times and the good, and in joy and sorrow. I promise to support you in your every decision, to treat you as an equal and to never force you to compromise in any situation."

Vanessa smiled at Kevin as he paused to especially gaze into her eyes, "Tomorrow is not always going to keep coming, so I promise to keep on loving you unconditionally for all the todays God might gift me with."

Lauren's eyes had trailed to Scarlet as she saw the dark-haired woman close to tears while staring at her sister and her brother-in-law.

Just as Kevin's vows ended, Vanessa laughed nervously, "Oh wow, I'm sorry, but I forgot all of my vows." Kevin laughed heartily as he shook his head at his wife. "Say anything." He spoke lovingly, gazing at her.

And Vanessa did just that, "I, Vanessa Ava Payne, take you, Kevin James Anderson, as my lawfully wedded husband, friend and lover for as long as I am alive. I promise to be your armor when this world is too cruel in its attacks, to be your anchor when you feel like you can't live anymore, and to be your balloon to keep you afloat and above the world at all times."

Kevin chuckled as Vanessa blushed before continuing, "In front of my dysfunctional family, and idiotic friends, I give you my word to love you unconditionally and without doubt. I will forever stay loyal and faithful to you, well, as long as you are the same with me too. Because if you aren't, I think I'll get too angry and murder you at the spot."

The priest gave Vanessa a look of disbelief as he shook his head. "Sorry." Vanessa apologized before she bowed her head.

"The rings please."

Gregory was pushed forward by Juliet, as he was beside her.

The two rings, made of pure platinum with letterings engraved in them, were presented to the bride and the groom.

Vanessa was the first one to place the ring on Kevin's finger before he did the same, all the while with dopey smiles on their faces.

"Speak now or forever hold your peace." The priest waited as everyone smiled and no one stood up dramatically yelling 'Wait!', before he continued,

"In the power invested in me, I pronounce you husband and wife. You may now kiss the husband."

"Wait, isn't that supposed to be..." Kevin was cut off when Vanessa tipped him and planted her lips onto his own, while loud cheers erupted from their family and friends.

"Finally!" Juliet shouted as she raised her hands in the air.

Yes, finally, indeed.

The clinks of glassware and buzz of talking was hard to avoid as Lauren forced Scarlet into making a toast.

Scarlet, who was in no way wanting to make a toast, frowned before she clinked her glass a little too hard, making it sound like a battle warning. "Sorry." She spoke the first word as everyone's attention was now settled on her.

"I wanted to make a toast to my sister and brother-in-law." Vanessa awed from her seat beside Kevin at the top of the stage.

"First of all, I'll pray for your life every day, man, because living with her is like surviving deadly bombs. You don't know where one might come from." Everyone laughed while Vanessa glared at Scarlet.

Lauren pinched Scarlet's side harshly as she glared at her as well.

"Sorry again." Scarlet mumbled, loud enough for everyone to hear, before she continued, "Second of all, if you don't keep her happy, you already know what might happen to you. And by the way, we all were born and raised as assassins."

"Oh, my god." Vanessa hid her face with her hand as Kevin laughed from beside her.

"And lastly, you might not be a blood brother to me but, as long as you keep my sister happy, I'll pretend that you're my brother from another mother." Raising her glass in the air, Scarlet smiled and sat down.

It was deathly silent in the hall as everyone looked at Scarlet in awe. "Wow, I thought, you'd only talk nonsense." Lauren spoke in disbelief as she smiled at Scarlet, who shrugged with a cheeky grin.

"You got to get the people in the mood before throwing gushiness at them."

Lauren chuckled as she slapped Scarlet's arm before resting her head on her shoulder with a sigh, "I'm so happy right now."

"I am too." Scarlet sighed back as she grabbed Lauren's hand, with the intention of never letting go.

"Hey, do you want to ditch this joint?" Scarlet spoke up after a minute and Lauren immediately raised her head from her shoulder to look at the older woman with a look of disbelief. "Are we even allowed to do that?"

"No one will know. Besides, I wanted to take you somewhere."

Lauren looked around at the Payne family, talking and eating away. Surely, they wouldn't notice if Lauren and Scarlet just disappeared. And besides, it wasn't their wedding party.

Lauren nodded before Scarlet smiled and grabbed her suit jacket from the back of her chair, holding out a hand for Lauren to take.

They snuck out of the hall with giggles pouring out of them and smiles as wide as they could go, and hands intertwined together like vines.

"There they go." Juliet spoke as she smirked towards Blake, "Pay up, ding dong." Blake frowned before he grumbled and got a 50-dollar bill out from his pocket.

"You really are a ding dong, it was completely predictable that they would just up and leave as if they were invisible or as if we're dumb." Claire chuckled as she sipped her drink.

"Or blind." Hayden piped in as she leaned back in her chair.

"Oh come on, let them have their fun." Josh spoke as he patted Blake's back with sympathy.

"Yeah, the fun that you two have whenever you're alone." Jordon smirked as he pointed at the two lovers. Josh blushed immediately, while Clayton nodded shamelessly.

"At least, we don't do it where people eat." Clayton remarked as he gave Kyle and Allison a pointed look.

"Oh please, you two basically had your hands in each other's pants at Aunt Carrie's wedding." Claire smirked as she remembered the time.

Hayden laughed with a nod as she bumped her shoulders with a smirking Clayton, who bumped back.

"Sheesh, you people nasty." Juliet spoke and the whole table erupted with laughs.

"Poor Stewart." Lauren giggled as they got into Stewart's car. "he might never forgive you for this crime."

Scarlet laughed as she put the car in reverse and out of the parking lot, "I don't want him to forgive me, not now at least."

"So, where are we going?" Lauren asked after they had come onto the main road. "Are we going back to the house?"

Scarlet glanced at the blonde as she smirked, "Why? Anything you want to do there without the family, in the dark?"

Lauren blushed as she slapped Scarlet's arm, making the older woman laugh in response.

"Don't worry, we aren't going there, but someplace else."

"Where?" Lauren asked and Scarlet shook her head.

"You'll see."

Lauren only groaned before slumping back into her seat.

"Here we are." Scarlet spoke as she parked the car in front of a small ice cream parlor. "An ice cream parlor?" Lauren questioned as she turned to look at her lover.

"Yeah, come on." Scarlet got out of the car and Lauren followed her lead after a second of contemplation.

Scarlet grabbed Lauren's hand and entered the ice cream parlor with a huge smile on her face, before going to the ordering area.

"Hi, what would you like to order, ma'am?"

Scarlet smiled politely at the woman before she spoke, "An ice cream sundae please."

Lauren's eyes widened and she stared at her lover, "What flavor?" The man behind the counter asked politely and Scarlet frowned before turning to the blonde.

"What flavor do you like?"

"Why are you doing this?"

Scarlet smiled before she squeezed the blonde's hand gently.

"Well, my new girlfriend is a model in New York, and since I'm almost broke and unemployed, I thought that maybe Stewart would want me back. Turns out, he was desperate enough to fall to his knees and give me his car for the rest of my life, just to get me back."

Lauren giggled, already imagining her brother doing that.

"So, I took the job back, just to be close to my hot girlfriend. Whose gonna be there to protect her from lecherous people if not me?" Lauren smiled before she threw herself at her, instantly breathing in the smell of safety and security, as well as strawberries.

"I like strawberries."